# SEVENTEEN GRAMS OF SOUL
## EMILIO DEGRAZIA

### LONE OAK PRESS, LTD.

To Monica Drealan DeGrazia, my best
and sometimes only reader, my wife
and passionate friend.  Her attention
to detail and the quality of her judgment
have been especially valuable
over the years.

SEVENTEEN GRAMS OF SOUL

BY

EMILIO DEGRAZIA

PUBLISHED
BY
LONE OAK PRESS, LTD.
304 11TH AVENUE SOUTHEAST
ROCHESTER, MINNESOTA 55904-7221
507-280-6557    FAX 507-280-6260

**First Edition**

ISBN NUMBER 1-883477-07-7
LIBRARY OF CONGRESS CARD CATALOG NUMBER 94-072988

Several of the short stories in this collection have been previously published. We gratefully acknowledge permission to reprint slightly altered versions of them here:

"The Girl in the Yellow Dress" (*Santa Clara Review*, 1991); "The Trip around the Moon" (*Madison Review*, 1988, reprinted in *Northfield Magazine*, 1992); "Seventeen Grams of Soul," (*The Bridge*, 1992); "Translations" (*Kansas Quarterly*, 1989); "A Minnesota Story" (*The Minnesota Experience*, Adams Press, 1979; reprinted in *Red Cedar Review*, 1979); "Reunion" (*Exquisite Corpse*, 1993); "Godspeed" (*Muscadine*, 1992); "Nine-Tenths of the Law" (*North Dakota Quarterly*, 1994).

We also gratefully acknowledge permission to reprint the excerpt from Robert Leckie's *Deliver Us from Evil: The Saga of World War II* (Harper and Row, 1987) as "Historical Note on 'War Stories.' "

Cover art by Mary Tambornino, Minneapolis,
Cover design by Teri Goff, Elba, Minnesota.
Black and white drawings by Julia Crozier, Bellevue, Iowa.
Photograph by Emily De Grazia, St. Paul, Minnesota.

Emilio De Grazia is a Fiscal Year 1992 recipient of a Fellowship grant from the Minnesota State Arts Board, through funds provided by the Minnesota State Legislature.

# CONTENTS

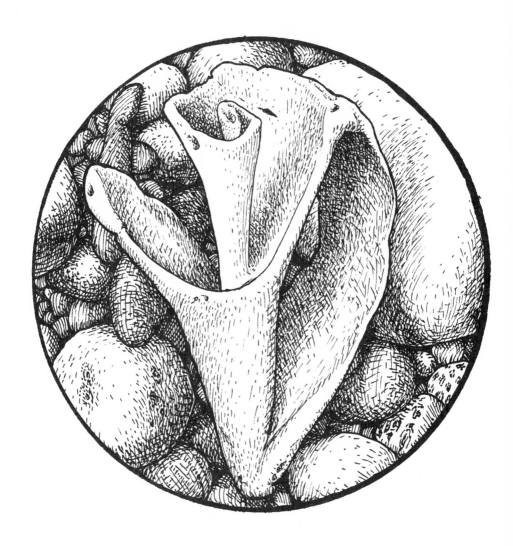

# THE GIRL IN THE YELLOW DRESS

Ruth's younger brother Ben, still unable to believe that her end was just weeks away, helped her to a front row seat in the lecture hall just as Stephen Hawking, the renowned physicist twisted in a wheelchair by disease, was about to explain the meaning of time. From the moment the lecture began she concentrated her gaze on the young genius and held it there until he concluded his talk. Afterward it was clear that she had committed some of his words to memory. "Imagine," she said as her brother helped her out. "He thinks time-travel is really possible through black holes in space. You could go through a black hole and return before you had left, or maybe use a black hole to travel back in time and kill your parents before you were born." Her eyes narrowed as she stared into space. "Imagine that."

A month later, too weak to leave her bed, she still stared into space, not with that blankness full of dread but with the same strange intensity. Ben had come back six hundred miles to spend a few days with her, each day lengthening into long bedside hours that gave him more than enough silence to fill with memory and regret. Content over the years to let the birthday card, Christmas gift, and holiday call take care of family business, he had never opened his heart to her. Now, as the curtain was about to fall, he was afraid to speak his lines in their final act. The decorum of death confused him into a paralysis. Was he to speak only when spoken to, or carry on as if there were nothing the matter at all? Now that her life was contracting to its final intensity, curling like a leaf protecting itself from the sun, how small should his talk be? And what right and obligation did he have to urge from her any final soliloquies, presume to record her last will and testaments? Was it perhaps better to be entirely evasive of the "Thing" consuming her, particularly if the evasions, if entertaining enough, had any power to distract and thereby slow the Thing's approach?

The usual preliminary pleasantries were hardest, the silence that followed eventually embarrassing him into the words that came forth before he could stop to consider their appropriateness.

"What is it – the most vivid thing that happened to you?" he asked out of the blue of a sunny afternoon.

Her eyes darted toward him and then resumed their distant stare. Immediately he wanted to take his words back, afraid that his question assumed that she had nothing to look forward to but the review of a life already spent. The thought troubled him more because he considered her life ordinary and dull. Along with her two children, uneventfully raised and sent off to colleges, she had settled for routine accomplishments, experiencing the daily sadness and perks common to a wife in a house. True, she had seen a bit of the world, but always as a vacation of the house that seemed emptier when she returned to it, never as an adventure that made her life take off.

As Ben waited for a response, he imagined his words circling the room in search of a place to alight. He was surprised when she began a measured and clear response.

"There was a girl once," she said almost inaudibly, "in a yellow dress. We both were young then. She was pretty – long brown hair and dark eyes – and she always stood apart. It was a Sunday morning and her dress was trimmed in lace and the sky was all blue. Standing there outside the church, everyone seeing how pretty she was. I asked if she wanted to go in with me, and she didn't know. She was angry and sad. I went inside, and when I looked back I saw her walking away from the church. I never saw her again."

"What was her name?" Ben asked.

"Her name? It's funny how you forget. It's as if she never had a name of her own."

Aware that her hours were like a handful of change being spent one coin at a time, he wondered why her memory opened so generously to the girl in the yellow dress. And Ruth had been religious, indeed devout, all her life. Why such a strong and sympathetic attachment to a girl whose moment in life occurred when she walked away from a church?

"What was she thinking about?" he asked.

"She was thinking big. She had made up her mind to change the world."

Ben suppressed his cynicism. "How far did she get with that?"

"Doesn't the world change when we change our way of looking at it?" his sister said as she closed her eyes and turned away.

❧❧❧❧

Immediately after the diagnosis was first confirmed the conversation had taken the expected turn.

"No, I haven't called them yet," she said to Ben over the phone. "I've been too scared to tell Mom and Dad. This will kill them before it kills me."

"They'll want to come here to be with you."

"That's the worst part of it. They'll come all that way and then they'll worry and stay. And Mom – you know how she is – will be hysterical and begin driving me insane. She's never wanted to let go of either you or me, and she'll act as if what's happening to me is the end of the world."

"Do you want me to call them... to explain?"

"No. I'll call them myself. And don't tell the kids."

The change took hold long before her body began to fail in any visible way.

"There comes a time," she announced that same week, "when you really begin caring about what people think."

She began with the kitchen cupboards and worked her way through the house, every wall and floor scrubbed, every piece of furniture moved so she could get to corners untouched for years. She turned to the basement next, carting off boxfuls of junk and polishing the vinyl floors. Her appetite for work, as if taking nourishment from the virulent new cells multiplying within, grew even as she concluded her long-unfinished projects around the house. Nights she turned to her quilt, begun after her first child was born then set aside for the rainy days that seldom came as her children ran in and out of the house for years. When spring arrived she took to the yard – the hedges first, then the flowers and grass, all carefully weeded and trimmed.

"Now then," she said as she stood on the sidewalk contemplating her house, "all it needs is a bit of paint."

"I had no idea she'd go this far," her husband Dick complained to Ben. "She wants everything just so. When I ask her to slow down she just gets that long look in her eye and I figure there's no more arguing with her. I guess she needs to keep busy to keep her mind off this thing that's happening."

Ben gave her more credit than that. Her busy-ness distracted her more effectively than idleness did, but it was order, he concluded, that she mainly was working toward. As the disease ate its way into the fabric of her life, she needed to salvage and restore what she could. Any order would do – a house freshly painted and washed clean, a yard full of normal blossoming things, a quilt stitched together to cover a body disintegrating by night. We must allow her that, he told himself –

5

any little tidiness her heart desires now, any new order to make time stand at attention, salute, and obey.

Then one day he received a call from Dick.

"I don't know what to do," Dick said. "She's acting weirder now. She's emptying all the closets and drawers in the house."

"What's wrong with that?"

"This isn't spring cleaning we're talking about. She's gone through my files and burned all the tax records and receipts. Taxes are due in a week and I've tried to fill out new forms, but she refuses to sign."

"Because they're not... accurate?"

"Of course they're accurate," he lied. "She says she doesn't like how the taxes are spent – says she's been waiting all her life to do his kind of thing."

ᴁᴁᴁᴁ

Perhaps because he was her brother he had never looked closely at her skin before. As a boy he thought she was pretty enough, even beautiful when he paused to imagine her, and until she got married he kept thinking of her as pretty and young. But right after her wedding he began feeling the sullen contempt he saw in the silences her husband locked her in. She was letting herself go, gaining weight, wasting her life, and Dick had good reason to be turned off. Much later, when the disease first became visible, Ben noticed the way her eyes, though more wary and alert, seemed to be shrinking back, the circles surrounding them like bruises on skin that suddenly seemed ashy and pale. A few days after her treatments ended a new color appeared, an orange flush that promised a new blossoming even on skin that was beginning to drape from her frame. Within a week the orange faded, leaving behind a jaundiced hue.

One week before she died he again was at her side, relieved to find her head turned away and her eyes closed. It took him minutes to realize she was not asleep, and when she turned his way he was surprised by the power in her voice.

"I thought you were somewhere else," she began. "I was about to call."

"I've been here all the time."

"Something's on my mind."

The Thing, he thought, for it would not leave him in peace.

"You remember the girl, the one I was telling you about. I never finished telling about her."

6

"About how she wanted to change the world."

She closed her eyes a moment and smiled.

"She took lovers, lots of them."

"At such a young age? How old did you say she was – thirteen?"

"Yes," she smiled again. "She was ready for them, certainly ready for 'It' by that time, though she couldn't understand the nature of the thing she had spent thirteen years getting ready for."

"So she abandoned everything – walked away from the church?"

"Yes, and home."

"With some boy five years older?"

"Eventually she got bored with them, the lovers, got rid of them one by one just like the jobs she had to put up with just to get on."

"Did she ever marry?"

"Not in any usual sense." She turned toward the window as she closed her eyes and began slipping into sleep.

"Do you think she's in great pain?" Dick asked after Ruth fell asleep, his own face showing the strain of their extraordinary past six months.

"Pain? There has to be a lot of pain. She's been keeping a lot from both of us for a long time now."

"Well, it's not been easy on me either, you know."

"Right now her problems look more serious to me."

"It's easy enough for you to say – because you're not living with her day in and day out. It's like she isn't my wife anymore. You have no idea of how strange she's become."

"What could be more strange than what she's going though?"

Dick dismissed the comment with a shrug. "When this whole thing started," he said, "I made up my mind to make it as comfortable as possible for her, do everything I could. But you could hardly call her behavior cooperative."

"Cooperative?"

"You're in the dark about a lot of things. Yes, cooperative."

"And what is the nature of my ignorance?"

"You don't know, for example, about the telephone calls. Long-distance calls – to her friends. Even old high school friends she hasn't heard from in God only knows how many years. Dozens and dozens of calls, and not for a few minutes to explain about herself but sometimes for an hour or two just to talk."

There had always been a bottom line to Dick's complaints: He paid the bills.

7

"Seems as if she has some rights, especially now. It all seems normal enough to me."

"Because you don't know the half of it. If it was just a thousand dollar phone bill for a few months I could live with it. But you don't know about the necklace she gave away to a niece, and God only knows what else from our safety deposit box, and the checks she writes to charities and her church. It's as if I'm not going to be around to pick up the pieces after she's gone."

The brother-in-law rose up in Ben. "Has it occurred to you that maybe she's trying to catch up with lost time?"

"I couldn't blame her if that was the case," he replied, "because that's what I'd do too, go out and just have a blast. But I think that disease has touched her in the brain. I don't think she's quite all there anymore."

"My sister is not insane."

"Then why does she keep trying to call the President of the United States, raising her voice, trying to give him a piece of her mind? I've walked in on her lots of times with her on that phone talking to somebody in Washington, D.C. She goes on and on."

"That's not so strange," Ben said, "and not insane. Don't you go calling my sister insane."

Dick shook his head as if he did not hear Ben's words. "That's why I wonder," he said, "how much real pain she must be in. Why maybe it would be a blessing if God took her out of her misery."

ॐॐॐॐ

Later, Ben found her looking out the window again, the late afternoon light slanting in on the lower part of her bed. He took her hand and enclosed it in his own, a shudder moving through him as he felt how small the bones of her fingers were. He closed his eyes and thought of his women over the years, how someday he would marry one of them and perhaps hold her hand like this. When he opened his eyes he found her looking at him.

"Dick is afraid of me now," she said. "When he's here in the room he's always pacing back and forth."

"Is it you he's afraid of or what's happening to you?"

"It's disgust. He can't stand touching me."

"Here then," Ben said, squeezing her hand, "let me."

She opened into a faint smile. "Things are never easy for women, you know, even when they're beautiful and rich. It's something you may understand but never feel the way women do. You remember the girl in the yellow dress? She never did come back."

"You never found out what happened to her?"

"There were rumors, about her lovers mainly, but also about how she had come to fame or shame. We knew for sure that she had seen the world, or at least the better part of it, Paris at least. And some of her lovers turned cruel on her, forcing her to move on, sometimes hide. We heard she spent years as a waitress in an east Texas town, working at night toward some sort of college degree."

She turned toward him, drawing her hand away, her eyes narrowing with the intensity of her effort to recall.

"There was always that wild streak in her, you know. You could never tell how fast she was going where. She'd dance on tables in barrooms and run off to some weekend honeymoon with a man half her age. Her parents were always ashamed of her. They acted as if she were dead, even after they heard she maybe was doing wonderful things."

"So they never had a chance to reconcile?"

Her eyes circled, as if she were turning the question over in her mind.

"She knew they refused to forgive her, so they kept fading away from each other, especially as her traveling took her farther and farther away, eventually too far to return. Then one day they woke up and started looking for her whenever they went out of town, even though it had been so many years. They started looking for her eyes, the shape of her forehead, even that same pretty yellow dress they remembered her in. Yellow dresses on strangers walking by. And of course they begin seeing yellow dresses everywhere, and here the eyes, in another girl the way she used to walk, and then in a crowded restaurant or airport they get a glimpse of her wild and innocent look. Traces. Here and there and everywhere you see them when you're looking for someone you've lost. You want to stop these people, ask them their names, where they're going next, what they did right or wrong, not let them get away from you. But they do, you know, and you end up just standing there alone, watching them get small and more important as they walk away."

She propped herself up on an elbow and motioned for him to help her sit up. He was struck by how light she felt in his hands, her flesh like the nightgown covering her bones. She took a sip of water as he set a pillow behind her back, and once settled into his own chair he felt the weight of her body still on his hands.

9

That night he found himself behind the wheel of his car again, staring at the six hundred miles in front of him, a vast space that seemed to narrow and darken as the hours wore on, his sister's face, drawn and pale, before him the whole way, nearing, becoming clearer, kinder as he got closer to home. Dizzied by the long drive, he went straight to bed and slipped into disconnected dreams. When the phone rang he did not know where he was.

Her voice seemed distant and small, but he knew it immediately.

"I couldn't sleep," she said. "After I looked out the window and saw your car pulling away, all I could think of was you. Was I the older sister always nagging you?"

"No, you were always pretty and immature, never acting your age. We had just broken the window at the Harrison house and we were laughing and running away. Do you remember that – how we hid in the cellar, and we lied when Mom and Dad asked if we were the guilty ones?"

"I was eleven and you were nine."

"And we got married in the cellar the next day."

"I asked you to marry me."

"Then Mom and Dad found out we lied about the window."

"And I got all the blame."

"I was too young."

"You were the boy. Breaking windows was okay for you. And right now I have to worry about Dick."

"Why?"

"He doesn't want me making calls," she whispered, "especially to you."

He raised his voice. "There's no way he can... "

"Yes darling, I know that now. Besides, I've been more than fair with him. I'm taking the kids but leaving him the house. I got it all bright and clean for him. That seems fair enough."

෧෧෧෧

She refused all medications and visitors except Ben.

"In the left-hand drawer of my dresser," she said when Ben returned, "you'll find letters to all of my friends. Please deliver them at the appropriate time, and please make sure that the terms of my will are met. And I never did get through to the President, so maybe you could keep trying for me. And don't back down on any points. You know how strongly I feel about the way he's wasting our tax money on his death machines. And I've already told Dick that he'll need to get married again right away, so do keep an eye on him until he does."

That evening she called him to her bedside again. The light was dimming outside, her face a shadow in the room. She took his hand and looked past him until he was moved to look over his shoulder for someone else in the room.

"She wrote me once – from California. She had a few regrets, and California was her worst mistake. People there cared only about themselves, going from one thing to another thing – drugs, religions, shopping malls. But she wanted me to come there. And she wanted me to do a favor for her: Get in touch with her mother and dad and tell them she was okay. Not to worry about her. Would I do that, please?"

She pulled him in close and whispered.

"I suppose you want to know what it's like when it's actually happening. It isn't really much of anything. At first it's just a heaviness in the legs and you're tired all the time, like I'm a heavy shopping bag I have to carry around all the time. Then at night I begin sinking away. Leaves, grass, rain – everything goes through as if you're a sieve. Especially thoughts, some so beautiful I have to keep looking for them, lots of them swirling and swirling like water going down a drain, with me swirling after them. And the more I toss and turn the more light-headed and careless I get, and when the urge comes on to let go, just fall, then I feel as if I have the right to do anything I want, go anywhere, anytime, just fly.

"And that's how it goes with me. So would you do one more thing before you go. Would you dial for me? I want to tell Mom and Dad to come now. Would you do that for me, please, and then turn off that light?"

12

# WINDOW VOICE

It didn't take long for LeRoy Barney to get interested in Nora Barr. At his age he had seen too many houses suddenly go silent in the little Tampa neighborhood he and his wife Alberta had retired to years ago, so they both perked up when the green bungalow next door finally showed a "Sold" sign. And Nora Barr turned out to be something else. For more than three months she wore a track into her back yard lawn, carrying on conversations LeRoy could never quite hear. "And now that he's dead," LeRoy complained, "she's even worse. All those afternoons spent jabbering at her husband's grave. I bet she was a pretty good looker in her day. I don't know why she keeps carrying on like that."

Before Nora actually moved in both he and Alberta watched from behind the draped window in front, the trucks coming and going for three days, workmen unloading furniture, cartons, and things, things, things that seemed too much for the small bungalow to contain. On the last day a tow truck deposited its haul in front of the garage: A 1972 silver-grey Lincoln Continental as shiny as a new-minted coin. And a few minutes later a taxi pulled up and Nora stepped out, her face weary and nervous, her hands rummaging ineptly in her purse for the keys to her new home. "You have to wonder," LeRoy said as he watched Nora trying to fit the key in her door, "if she's going to have any room for herself in that house."

The very next morning Nora appeared outside the bedroom in back facing the Barney window over the kitchen sink. There she began her routine, the pacing back and forth on the lawn, the mumbling directed at the dark screen of the bedroom window facing the Barney house.

"She's crazy," LeRoy concluded after a week of it.

"She's not," Alberta replied. "She explained everything yesterday when you were asleep with your nap. Her husband's in there – in that back room. He's real sick, can hardly breathe. She has to take care of him, do what he says. His name is Frederick."

"Well that's that and it's too bad," LeRoy said as he stretched to close the window over the sink, "but I don't see why I have to put up with him too."

LeRoy was watering his bushes when Nora came over a second time. She approached gingerly, lifting the hem of her pink-flowered dress and pausing at the property line before stepping over it.

"I really shouldn't be doing this," Nora said as Alberta opened the back door for her. "Freddy's sleeping right now. He would kill me if he knew."

Alberta offered her a chair. "I was just going to put some coffee on."

"Oh no, I really can't stay," Nora said as she sat. "But these are such beautiful chairs."

As Alberta filled the coffee pot, Nora began telling her tale. She and Frederick were from Flint where he worked in the open hearth for thirty-seven years. And yes, there were kids, two sons, both married and gone. Florida seemed right after all those winters up north, so they returned to Tampa as soon as they could. And Frederick finally cut his smoking down to one pack a day. Then all the doctors told him the same thing – emphysema, a terrible disease. "He's confined to that bed," she said, "and we're rather beside ourselves these days."

"Is there anything we can do?" Alberta asked.

"Oh please, just half a cup," Nora said as Alberta poured, "and oh what beautiful cups." She held her cup to the light, then lowered her voice. "And your husband, he's such a handsome man. He can't be a day over sixty years old."

LeRoy, dousing the azaleas next to the patio, splashed some water on the screen. "You got coffee in there?"

"He's seventy-nine," Alberta replied.

"My, my, what a lucky girl you are," Nora mumbled over her cup. "He's such a good-looking man for his age."

LeRoy came in and circled the table before taking the chair across from Nora.

"So your husband's sick?" he asked as Alberta went to fetch the coffee pot.

"A bit under the weather again," Nora replied, not taking her eyes from the cup.

"Serious stuff?"

"Oh you know how it goes. He's so stubborn. He won't leave the room, won't even visit the doctor any more." She looked up and smiled. "He says they're all crooks, even the nurses these days.

Everyone's a crook. He has such a hard time talking, you know. He gets so red in the face."

"What's your husband going to do with that car in your driveway? You got it for sale?"

"Oh, I don't drive," Nora said. "Never did. That's Freddy's car."

"How much you asking for it?"

Nora's eyes grew wide. "Oh no, Freddy would kill me if I sold his car. But I just love these chairs."

"They're for sale," LeRoy said.

Nora ran her hand over the arm of her chair and moved in for a closer look. "Really? Really for sale?"

"So's the table. We were going to put in an ad, but we'll knock something off for you."

Nora looked over her shoulder toward the back bedroom window of her house. "How much?" she whispered.

"Two hundred twenty-five."

Alberta threw LeRoy a glance.

"Two hundred for you."

"Oh beautiful," Nora said, "But I can't do it, I just can't. We have a little savings but he doesn't want me buying anything now. He'd kill me if he found out. You say two hundred for everything?"

"I don't know how we could go any lower... "

Nora suddenly stood. "Ssh, I have to go. He's calling me." She put her foot on the chair and rolled down her sock. Inside was a wad of hundred dollar bills. She peeled off two and handed them to LeRoy. "Here, but you have to promise not to whisper a word. You keep everything here for now. I'll come back for it when I can. I have to go now. Love you. Bye."

LeRoy couldn't take his eyes off her ankles as she walked toward the door, and that night he was awakened in the middle of a dream by the sound of water shooting from a garden hose. When he went to the window to check, he saw Nora, her nightie half-dripping wet, wiping Freddy's Lincoln Continental with a white linen cloth.

❧❧❧❧

Eventually Alberta heard what Nora had to say. Her feet aching under the strain, she spent long minutes peering through the window over her kitchen sink. From inside the small black screen of the window next door Frederick's voice, a low raspy growl, came across to her.

"Nora, come in here right now and turn me around," were the first words Alberta thought she heard. When Nora stopped in her tracks, turned, and hurried into the house, Alberta was sure she could believe her ears.

"Every time I turn around," LeRoy complained, "you're just standing by the sink. Can't you think of anything else to do with your time?"

Alberta waited for LeRoy to turn his back, then strained even harder to hear what was being said next door.

One day LeRoy slammed the door as he entered the house. "There she goes again – at it again. I don't understand what she's blabbering about this time."

Alberta turned her back to the sink. "She says he wants her to clean the house again today, and he wants turkey casserole for dinner tonight. She should watch out for life insurance cheats, and no, she'd better not dream of sending him to some hospital because he won't give a pack of doctors the pleasure of robbing him of his life savings. And did she wash the car today? If either of his sons ever show their faces anywhere near his house, she should tell them both to go straight to hell. And no, like he said a thousand times, she doesn't need another dress."

"So okay," LeRoy said, "what did she say back?"

"She said, 'Sure, sure, it's okay.'"

"So when do we eat?"

They ate later than usual that night. By seven-thirty the roast wasn't quite done, LeRoy glaring from his chair at Alberta dragging her feet getting the table set. By eight-fifteen, when Alberta placed the platter on the table, the roast was too dry.

"See," LeRoy said as his jaws worked over a chunk of meat, "I told you it was overcooked."

The rap on the back door came just after the sun finally set. Nora took one cautious step in, her right hand nervously stroking her arm.

"He never wants me to go out," she whispered, "and you know I can never be sure if he's really asleep. And I haven't washed the car in three days, and he wants me to clean the house again tonight."

"Is there anything we can do?" Alberta asked.

"The chair. Can I take one of my beautiful chairs home tonight?"

ॐॐॐॐ

16

Nora came for her chairs one by one, carrying the last one off on the night Frederick died. LeRoy and Alberta, eager to get their first glimpse of the man they had known only as the low growl coming from the window facing their house, were among the first to visit the funeral home.

"Frankly, I wasn't very impressed," LeRoy said. "I didn't think he'd be bald or that short. I expected somebody else."

The morning after the funeral Nora resumed the pacing in her yard.

"She's still talking to him," LeRoy complained. "Isn't she ever going to stop?"

Alberta lowered her eyes and retreated from the sink. "What do you want for dinner tonight?"

From the living room window LeRoy studied the Lincoln Continental again. No sign of rust, no visible nick or scratch, and the tires almost new. The interior done in blue suede, the tinted windshield like the wide sunglasses teenage boys wear at the beach. And he loved the little round case for holding the spare. This was a beautiful car. Besides, he was tired of the Oldsmobile. And she didn't even drive. Maybe now she would make him a deal.

Nora, carrying a dozen red roses in one hand, appeared at the door just before dark.

"Aren't they beautiful?" she said, the sadness of the funeral still on her face. "I thought you might want to keep them for your house."

"Oh come in," Alberta said, "and stay a while."

Nora shrank back. "Oh no, I really couldn't do that. You know I really shouldn't be away from the house. There were so many flowers at the funeral parlor. I just couldn't imagine getting them all back here. We already have so many things, you know."

LeRoy appeared over Alberta's right shoulder. "What about the car? Is it for sale?"

"Oh no," Nora replied as she handed Alberta the roses. "I don't think he'd let me sell the car." Then she broke into a gentle smile. "But I'll ask about that too."

"The flowers are beautiful," Alberta said. "I wish you would have asked us to bring them home for you."

Nora smiled again. "Oh these weren't for the funeral. Mr. Flossom has them delivered to me every month. Now isn't that nice?"

"Mr. Flossom?"

"He owns the Garden Dress Shop. He says I'm one of his favorite customers."

LeRoy popped up again. "If that car is going to do nothing but sit in your driveway, when are you going to want that table of yours?"

Nora lowered her voice as she backed away from the door. "Oh no, I couldn't possibly have it yet. It's way too soon for anything like that."

As he watched Nora walk over the lawn to her door, the thought began criss-crossing LeRoy's mind: She's crazy enough. Maybe he should keep the table and return one of those hundred dollar bills. Then one day she would trade him the table for the car even up.

ও•ও•ও•ও•

They watched from their front window as Nora got in the taxi every day at noon, and they made a point of going to the window for her return at five. Each day the cab driver, a short burly man with thinning hair, took her by the arm to her front door and made a second trip to carry her packages inside.

"She's got all that stuff going in that house," LeRoy said, "but when do you ever see anything coming out? I don't think it's fair for her to store that old table with us. I have half a mind to send her a bill for that."

"Oh hush," Alberta said. "She might be listening."

The next afternoon after LeRoy went down for his nap Alberta called out his name to see if he would stir. Seeing no response, she walked right over to Nora in her yard.

"Oh yes," Nora said, "I visit him every afternoon. Of course I stop to get some flowers first. Would you like to step inside?"

As she entered Nora's house Alberta couldn't help glancing to see if she was being caught in the act. The house – packed with things guarded, it still seemed, by the low-growling presence behind the screen of the window in back – had been off-limits to everyone. Though Frederick was dead, he was present enough to make Alberta feel she was intruding on forbidden turf, and behind her LeRoy, though by now sound asleep for almost an hour, was also telling her not to enter there.

Nora led the way to a living room full of furniture piled high with things. Next to the window stood a high-backed chair and a lamp with its shade slightly askew. From the living room Alberta could see into the kitchen – a Formica table, a stack of cartons next to the refrigerator, a broom leaning against the stove, and two of her old chairs all alone against the wall.

"Oh my," Nora said with a weak smile, "you can see I'm not quite all moved in yet. Would you like a cup of tea?"

They sat on the chairs sipping tea. "Freddy worked so hard," Nora said, "that I never really saw much of him. He did overtime almost all the time to make our little nestegg come true, and when he came home I was already in bed, tired, you know, from doing the usual things around the house. I'd get up to make him a breakfast and lunch, and I'd see him off to work. The children went to school. And then he retired and here we are. The next thing you know he was sick. If you ask me, we made up for all our lost time. We spent all our time together these last dozen years. That's what he always said: We have to make up for lost time. Then we moved in here so we could save a little more. This house is smaller but it's nice, don't you think? And then because he wasn't up to it, he wanted me to do the little things."

She wiped her hands on her dress as she went to the stove for tea. She was shaky as she poured for Alberta, spilling a few drops on the floor.

"I'm always so careless," she said as she sat again, "and I'm always forgetting things. He says it's because I'm getting old, and I suppose it's just true, you know. But then I ask: Have I ever, even once, forgotten to bring you flowers? He doesn't know what to say, so he just looks the other way."

She stood and put her cup on the edge of the sink. "Come on, let me show you some of the things. You know he put a few dollars away every week. We're going to retire to Florida someday is what he always said. It was his dream."

She took Alberta to the china cabinet in the dining room. Her pride and joy was a collection of hand-painted cups. And there were dozens of porcelain thimbles, each one exquisite and unique, their colors reflected in an antique cut glass decanter. "I started in collecting these," she said, "when he found out about the cups. But then he found out about the thimbles too."

There was silverware, tarnished but fine, and embroidered linen handed down for generations, and an old vase she bought at a garage sale for twenty-five cents. "I told him it was a steal," she went on, "and he agreed. And sometimes he went along with me, though I never could figure it out."

She tugged at Alberta's sleeve as she led her to a pile of old newspapers near the basement steps. "Ssh," Nora said. "Nobody will ever be able to say he wasn't looking after me. Here, look here."

At random she pulled out one of the old newspapers and unfolded it. Inside were three one-hundred dollar bills.

"That's just the way he was," Nora went on. "He never let me throw anything away. I swear you can't go anywhere in this house without finding one of his little surprises tucked away. Ssh. Can you imagine what's in that garage? Can you imagine what I found one night in one of his cigar boxes filled with nuts and bolts?"

She took Alberta by the hand. "Now you can't say a word. I'm going to show you what's in my room."

Her bedroom was across the hall from the one facing Alberta's kitchen, a hall heaped so high with cartons that Alberta hardly noticed, as she stole a glimpse through the half-opened door, that Freddy's bed was still unmade. Nora, leading her by the hand all the way, let go when the two of them stood next to her bed. "See," she said, "this is my room. I could hear him no matter what, even when our doors were closed."

Nora's room was tidy and prim, the lacy curtains on her window matching the fringe on her bed. Next to the bed was a small walnut table and a reading lamp.

"What a lovely little room," Alberta said.

"Oh thank you. I'm still tidying up the place."

Nora tugged at Alberta's sleeve once again and opened the closet door. Piled in stacks that rose to the ceiling were boxes full of new clothes.

"Mainly dresses," Nora said, a wide smile on her face as she pulled three boxes out. "He never came in here. Should we try one on?"

She put the boxes on the bed and opened all three. "Here," she said, "you choose. We're about the same size."

Alberta hesitated, then picked a blue and white chiffon, its price tag and labels still attached. Nora was already admiring herself in the mirror on the back of her door, holding against herself a mauve floor-length gown. "I wanted this one for a long, long time," she said as she smoothed it down over her hip.

Nora returned from the closet with a stack of boxes in her arms. When they emerged from the bedroom both were giddy from their laughing and talk.

"Now you have to take at least three home with you," Nora said.

"I couldn't do that. I just couldn't do that."

"You have to," Nora said as she steadied the boxes in Alberta's arms. "Because tomorrow I'm going to ask him for another one. I ask, you know, when I visit him, and sometimes he says go ahead. He's always taken care of me. So I really shouldn't be having these. And you look so good in them they seem all you. Besides, I don't really know what to expect. There's the grandfather's clock. I'm really pushing for that, but he just laughs whenever I bring that up. What am I going to do with a grandfather's clock? And yesterday Mr. Flossom took me to see the most beautiful one in my life – with three different chimes. So it's hard asking him for anything now, especially something big like getting rid of the car. I've got no real use for it. You could have it for nothing as far as I'm concerned, because I don't even drive. But whenever I bring up the subject of the car he has one of his fits. So we'll have to wait and see on that, and you just *have* to take these dresses out of here. You just do."

Alberta found herself standing at her own back door wondering if LeRoy was awake. What if he sees me with these dresses, she thought. What will I say? She thought of a place: Behind the water heater under the basement steps. He would never think to look for them there.

ঔ•ঔ•ঔ•ঔ

"I don't see why she doesn't stay home," LeRoy said as he glared at the taxi waiting in front of Nora's house. "She goes out every day."

"She visits him," Alberta replied, "takes him flowers, talks to him."

"Lots of good talking to a dead man does. She's out of her mind."

"You never know. She keeps asking him if it's time to get rid of the car."

LeRoy arched his left eyebrow. "Well I hope she makes some sense when she talks."

"Oh yes," Nora said the next day when she met Alberta at the property line, "we had another long talk today. He said I should wait until Saturday for another dress, and I agreed to only one. But he keeps saying no to the grandfather's clock. Where would we put it, he says, with the house already so full? I told him it had three different chimes but you can turn them off during the night so nobody wakes up. He says he doesn't care and we just sit and stare. Then he asks if I really *need* the thing. I've got a half-dozen watches and lots of clocks in all the rooms. I told him: You want me to stare all my life at *those* things? So what does he do? He changes the subject on me. One thing leads to another thing and I'm working up to ask about the car. 'Here,' I say, 'here's the flowers I brought you today. Aren't they

21

beautiful?' He just looks at them and then I get the feeling it's time to go. He's getting in one of his moods."

"Well it's very interesting," LeRoy said that same afternoon, "how that cab driver looks so much like her Freddy-boy. Did you ever notice his hair and how he waits on her hand and foot? Don't you wonder what *he* wants?"

"Probably," Alberta said, "he wants that car out of her driveway once and for all."

"What? What did you say?"

"Oh nothing."

"Nothing? That's what you think. Where do you think they really go every day? I'll tell you one thing: I don't see why she'd ever want to get into that cheap little taxi with him."

"And sometimes," Nora said to Alberta on a Sunday evening, "I don't know what to think. Yesterday I went to Mr. Flossom's again and he was so patient with me. I must have tried on a dozen or more and he really did help me decide. And he had them delivered that very night. And what else do you think? A lovely bouquet of flowers with a nice little note. So this morning I didn't stop at the flower shop. They were still so beautiful and fresh I took them along and set them down right in front of him. He didn't even look at them. At first I thought he was angry about the dresses again, and I was about ready to say I would take them back, but then I saw it was the flowers. He just stared and stared as if there was something wrong with them. And I was going to ask him about the car again. What do you think I should do?"

"Maybe," Alberta said in her sweetest voice, "maybe Mr. Flossom needs a nice car like that one you've got no use for any more."

"And how are we ever supposed to get a new table," LeRoy asked later that day, "if that old one is still in the house? Just look at that thing, all the nicks and scratches on those beat-up legs. I think we should give her a deadline. That's what I think."

"I don't think that would be very nice," Alberta said.

On the following Friday Alberta could see that Nora was down.

"I asked about the grandfather's clock today."

"What did he say?" Alberta asked.

"Nothing. He didn't say one word to me today."

めめめめ

22

For the next ten days they kept looking out the windows for some sign. Nora made no rounds on the path worn into her backyard lawn, and no cab driver appeared in front at the appointed hour.

"I don't like the looks of this," LeRoy said as he peered again through the front window drapes. "Something fishy's up."

"I wouldn't worry too much," Alberta said. "All the lights are on every night in the house. Maybe she's getting all her things sorted out. Besides, I saw her out late last night setting out the trash."

"I still don't like the looks of it."

LeRoy was beside himself the very next day when he burst in on Alberta frying him some eggs.

"I told you!" he screamed. "It's gone! The car is gone!"

"Well it certainly couldn't sit there forever."

"It was there last night before I went to bed. I'm sure of it. Would you go over and talk to her?"

Alberta flipped the eggs. "You expect me to leave the eggs?"

LeRoy refused to eat. He went to the window again and glared at the empty space in Nora's driveway, and then he went to the mailbox, pacing back and forth near the curb, looking up expectantly whenever a car neared. Finally he returned to the house and sat in his chair with his head in his hands.

Mr. Flossom appeared the next day, emerging unsteadily from the taxi that dropped him off in front of Nora's house. LeRoy and Alberta, standing back from their window in the shadows cast by the late afternoon sun, had to crane their necks to get a clear view of him.

"It's him for sure," Alberta said. "I was just in his shop last week."

"Just look at him," LeRoy mumbled. "Dark blue pinstripe suit. White carnation sticking out of a button hole. Standing there stiff as some fool sawed-off two-by-six. He looks like an undertaker to me."

Mr. Flossom disappeared inside and did not come out that night until after LeRoy had fallen asleep in his chair.

"Just think of it," LeRoy said as he opened his eyes to the Sunday morning singing of birds. "His body ain't warm in the grave, and already she's letting someone move in on her."

When Mr. Flossom arrived in the Lincoln Continental later that day, LeRoy watched helplessly. Mr. Flossom wore the same suit, but this time he was carrying a bouquet of roses under his arm. Nora made him wait before answering the door, and they spent a long minute talking before she let him in. When they came out again she was wearing an entirely different dress, this one lacy and pink, with ruffles in back. She gave him the keys to lock her door, but he handed them back as he held the car door open for her, both of them pausing so long to take in the scent of orange blossoms in the air that they could not have dreamt what LeRoy was saying to Alberta as Mr. Flossom put the car in gear and lurched away from the curb. And when Nora returned she found the old table upside-down on her lawn in back, just inches on her side of the property line.

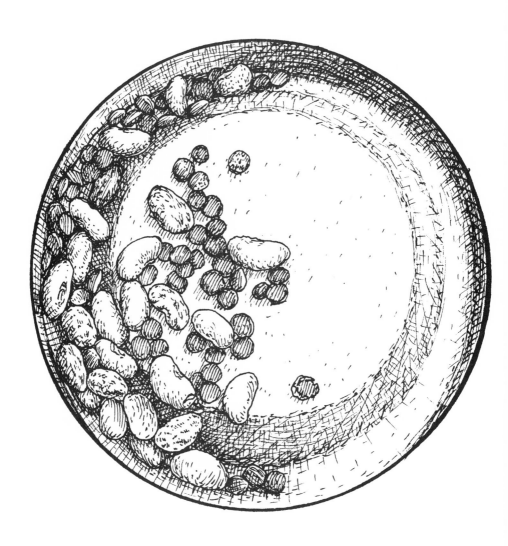

# SEVENTEEN GRAMS OF SOUL

For years Dr. Willard, cancer specialist, entertained wrong thoughts. The Laws of Conservation of Energy and Matter, reluctantly memorized for a high school science class, stayed with him as if they had been inscribed on tablets of stone. Later, when scientists revised the laws, he could not abandon the originals. With his work always running away from him he was content to let some things sit still in his mind. And there was another notion he could not abandon once it caught his eye. From a popular journal he had learned that seventeen grams of a typical human body's elemental weight could not be accounted for at the moment of death. According to the calculations of the reverend doctor who had researched the problem, this absence proved the existence of the soul.

Too often in his work he found the balance weighted in favor of depression and death. There had to be some reason for believing that a balance was not only possible but natural, that all would finally come to more than naught. If matter and energy could not be destroyed – if the drama called Life was the result of the way they traded masks – then balance was natural. And if seventeen grams of soul could survive, so too could a bit of hope.

Too often he stood back from his notions and saw how they missed the mark. True, they were superstitious errors that had no business in the mind of a scientist and professional. They were the unforced errors of the enthusiastic amateur – the kind that as a young man on the tennis courts he often had committed when, showing his very best form, he hit strong and beautiful shots that went out of bounds by no more than an inch. He could take a bit of pride in such errors, especially if they recurred with some consistency. They did neither him nor anyone else any real harm, for he had his private way of keeping score. Besides, he was careful to keep his ideas entirely to himself.

When his wife of forty-two years died in her sleep he felt cheated out of his chance to make things up to her. Though he had premeditated his own dying as a common and inescapable fate, he had never vividly imagined hers. Therefore hers seemed uncalled for, absurd. When he opened his eyes that frozen February morning to the strange stillness next to him in the bed, he again saw in her face the calm beauty that had lured him the very first time he saw her on the tennis courts. No wonder then that he pulled the blanket over himself and curled up closer to her, dozing off while her body, as if passing its life into him, slowly turned cold.

For weeks afterward he would sit up in bed in the middle of the night, reliving the shudder that finally woke him that day. He missed her just as he had missed out on her, especially after promising himself an early retirement full of voyages and dining out intended to set things right. Troubling hours he staved off by going to work earlier than usual and staying late. It was a strategy that had worked before, particularly when his wife had asked him to spend more time with her. And it worked again when he suddenly found himself old enough to retire. His colleagues dared not press the issue on a man so devoted and professional.

Work wearied him enough to deny him sleep. Every night just before turning off the light he glanced at the photo of his wife on the nightstand next to his bed. She still seemed soft in the dim light, but her smile seemed fixed on the window and its drawn shade, her face unmoved by his motions in the room. In the dark she seemed so effortlessly awake while he tried so hard to fall asleep.

When he first laid eyes on Mrs. Strom he did not catch her first name. Pert and slender, she wore a tight-fitting suit that hid none of her clear and well-proportioned lines. She dazzled even in the efficient office light, her hands brilliant with rings and her eyes and lips well-defined by makeup carefully applied. He quickly scanned his chart. She was forty-five, a Methodist, from a Minneapolis suburb, a widow, teacher and artist. And her cancer was incurable.

He did not know for sure when all her words began getting through to him. He asked the questions he was bound to ask, performing his routine, recording her responses and making his notes, her words not as clear or present as she was beautiful sitting in the chair a few feet from him. When he again had to look away from her, the words came through like a voice in a crowded restaurant. One clear sentence – "Should I ask him if it's terminal?" – required him to look up from his chart. He wanted to respond, No, please, don't ask me that, but held off, watching her instead as she lowered her eyes and folded her hands in her lap. From then on he evaded her questions one by one, sinking into sadness as he described in detail the side-effects of a variety of pills for relieving pain. Yet at the end of the interview when he stood at the door and offered her his hand he could not recall what pills he

26

had prescribed. She was not looking at him when she asked: "Does the good doctor really think these pills will be worth our while?" All he could see was the calm confidence and the life that came into her eyes as he heard himself say what he did not believe: "Yes, yes, of course there's hope for you."

As her second office visit approached he caught himself checking the calendar, each day lengthening as the appointment neared. He saw her more clearly this time, recalling her form and the fine lines of her face. As the hour approached he paced in his office looking for a way out of the meeting with her. He had been through it all before a hundred, a thousand, times. "What can I say?" he asked himself aloud. Her cancer was virulent and had begun to spread. As she grew weak she would begin to feel the force of his cheerful lie. What would he say when she felt her strength draining from her? Would he repeat the script used so many times before, the phrases so carefully prepared to announce that death was an inevitable short matter of time? As he imagined her he felt that his old words would not do, that she, dazzling and fine as she was, required an original response, words truer and better than any phrases he had used before. As the nurse led her in he feared that all words would fail him utterly.

She took her seat next to him, folded her hands in her lap and sat as one posing for an artist in the room. Already he saw the ashen discoloration of her skin. But the makeup on her face still seemed sharp and bright, the lines and shadows carefully brushed like those on a wonderful ballroom mask. Except for her small black eyes darting about the room, she sat motionless until he spoke.

"And how are you today, Mrs. Strom?"

He knew what she would say to him: Now she was sure about what was happening to her, the fatigue weighing her down, the discoloration of the skin, the nausea morning and night. She knew it was all over for her, just a matter of time. And she, because she knew he had feelings too and hated more than anything having to pronounce a death sentence on anyone, would not ask him for any official word.

"I think we'll be all right," she replied.

She would prefer, then, to pretend not to know. This was the best, the most logical course, the one that kept her tied to the rest of humankind. This way her time would be short but not fixed, the same doom and prospect faced by all people who saw their lives in the long view.

"Oh yes," he smiled, "I think we will."

27

She crossed her leg and shifted in her chair so that her body was half-turned away from him. He had seen many do the same thing on facing the worst, as if they were ashamed of the way their bodies were failing them, apologizing for imposing their ill presences on the rest of the world.

"We'll just have to go on," she said, "from day to day. There's nothing so wrong or unusual about that. People everywhere face troubles every day and a lot of them are much worse off than you or me."

"Yes," Dr. Willard said, "that's a very healthy way to look at things."

"Ah things," she said, "things. That's the hardest part. I spend the best twenty years of my life trying to make beautiful things, and then there's the problem of parting with them. They do so grow out of one, you know, even the little rebels that don't turn out just right, and maybe that's why it's so hard parting with them."

Suddenly Dr. Willard thought of a thing: The picture of his wife on the nightstand next to his bed.

"Yes," he said, "but there still comes a time when it's best to get rid of them for good."

"Yes, dear, I'm perfectly aware of that."

The word "dear" arrested him while she talked on. Why would she call him "dear"? Did she say that to everyone or to a special few? Had she begun to discern his desire for intimacy with her? He tried reviewing the term in his mind much as he had listened to the bell in the steepled church near his house, its resonance and tone more interesting than the dull fact of the tolling itself.

"I'm not quite sure what to make of it," she went on, "this feeling I have in my bones, especially in the morning and at night. It's a dull fatigue... as if I were lying down in the dead of summer and it was just too humid to move... as if my chest and legs were heavy with... humidity... and all the time my mind is perfectly alert and keeps running away with my thoughts, things that still need to be done, new projects, ideas, new things to make. And I want to leap out of bed and begin in the middle of the night, though I'm so tired all the time now, especially my legs. What do you make of it?"

He waited for her to turn his way but was grateful she kept staring at the wall on the other side of the room. It meant she was dying, but he could not face her with the words. He assumed his most professional tone.

"There are, of course, certain ways the body has of balancing things out. I won't go into the chemistry of this, but we've learned that the body has ways to conserve itself and its energies. You know about the conservation laws? When you're working too hard, or a lively mind like yours just wants to take off, the body has ways of... absorbing all the energy so your system can slow itself down... so you can re-strengthen yourself. It all balances out. Do you understand?"

"But darling I can't fall asleep," she said, still looking at the wall on the other side of the room, "and the next day the whole thing just starts over again except that I'm more tired than before."

Dr. Willard sat back in his chair and pretended to study his chart. She looked so very beautiful to him, her body so slender and firm. How many years had it been since he had held a woman, his wife, in his arms?

"Well, I'm not sure what to make of that. Are you active? Do you play a sport, tennis now and then? Besides, it's sometimes hard for us to be exactly sure. But we could try running a few more tests."

She sat up straight on the edge of her chair and addressed her words to the wall.

"Well, dear, now he says he's not really sure. So what do you think? He says he wants to run more tests. I'm personally tired of all these tests, but I'll go along with them if you think we should. But then I just get sick and tired of everything these days, so maybe my judgment's not as fine as you sometimes gave me credit for. So what should we do? What do you think I should tell him, George?"

She sat unmoved for a long moment before turning to face the doctor again.

"We'll do more tests," she said. "When should I see you again?"

Don't leave, his heart said as he looked at her. Don't leave me alone in this room.

かかかか

So she was talking to George. Dr. Willard waited for her to leave before he checked it out in her file. George, her husband, had died nine years ago.

He could not get her out of his mind. As he walked down sidewalks he was sure he saw her in the crowd across the street, and though he tried catching up she always disappeared. In his office he sat in his chair looking out the window as other women, some more young and beautiful, walked past. In bed he kept seeing her hands, perfectly folded in her lap, and he reviewed the way she sat turned away from him, as if posing for an artist on the other side of the wall.

What was he to make of her little conversations with George? They were strange, but she was exceptional. They were insane, but her talk was controlled and grounded in common sense. He put two and two together. Even if the human soul amounted to more than seventeen grams, her George would be invisible. Clearly George was present in some form, so her habit of turning toward the wall – toward "him" – had to be the function of an artistic mind, the result of her professional inclination to create a presence she could not really see. How clever of her, Dr. Willard thought, how extraordinarily imaginative. How well everything adds up.

He caught himself waiting by the clock and calendar. He would see her again on Friday at nine o'clock sharp, but first he would have to glance at the results of her tests. Already he knew too well what would appear there, the words and numbers charting the inevitable progress of cells, their appetite virulent, like the sexual energy of youth. Once more he envisioned their steady growth, their sudden geometric invasion overwhelming every part, the eventual general collapse, and the final settling into entropy, the cancer having nothing but itself to feed on until it too went the way of all flesh, the body then reducible to a handful of ashes, they the only visible form of the absent seventeen grams.

The word "love" occurred to him when he saw her standing at the office door. She had on a lovely blue dress and a necklace thick with gems. Again she dazzled, but this time also with her smile.

"Going to a party?" he asked as he eased her into a chair.

"Yes, we're going out to dinner and then to dance later tonight," she replied, brushing her dress down smooth with her hands.

Her remark, light-hearted and polite, grew on him as they chatted on. He imagined her in the corner table of an elegant restaurant, the linen tablecloth white, the champagne poured, the talk in whispers all around. Who was it she was whispering with? He saw himself looking at them from across the room, a jealous lover alone. Who was this man she was dining and dancing with?

"It may be," he said, "that you will have to give up dancing for a while."

She turned away from him and faced the wall again, tilting her head upward like a woman too proud to respond to an impertinent remark.

He suddenly felt betrayed. What business did she have crossing him? In withholding the truth from her he had provided her authoritative reason to believe that her life would go on indefinitely. Had he not seen others collapse when confronted with the fact that they would not outlive their disease, then watch the disease grow suddenly hungry from that day on? Was his lie not proof that he cared for her? He began to see himself by her side. He was sixty-seven years old. His days were numbered too. Together why couldn't they make the best of what little time was left to them?

"George says that's crazy," she said while facing the wall. "He says we should dance until we drop."

He felt some relief at this. His rival was only her invisible George, so she still might consent to dining with him.

"Well," he said, "maybe we should run a few more tests before we turn you completely loose to playing tennis on the first warm day that comes along. We don't want to rush anything, so we'd better go slow."

Keeping her eyes on the wall, she shook her head as if she did not quite understand.

"I know, George, that now you're going to say I told you that's what the doctor would say."

⁂

Sitting back in his chair, he let her go on. It was easy for George to say go ahead with more tests because it wasn't his body they were working on. He didn't know the pain, the pain. No, she wasn't at all sure about the the tests, and in fact she had serious doubts about the medical profession in general. Didn't he? Well, if he agreed shouldn't they just go home where at least she could be working on her art? A new inspiration had come to her just yesterday, in fact while she was thinking about that trip they took – something fresh and original, and she could hardly wait to get started on it. Yes, of course she still wanted to go out to dinner tonight, and she wouldn't miss the dancing for anything. And only if he insisted would she stay for the doctor's next round of tests, but no more after that. Could they agree on something once in a while?

When she stood to leave Dr. Willard felt himself shrink. She and her George had agreed to abandon him. She would go through her next battery of tests, have her last audience with him, then leave. He would never see her again. He groped for the only words that occurred to him.

"I know," he began, "that these must be difficult times for you. "If there's anything I can do... to make my presence a comfort... "

She saved him from having to say more. "Oh don't you go worrying yourself about me."

"I mean... "

"Thank you," she smiled, "but no. I'm already busy tonight."

After she left he went to the wall where her George had appeared. The paint, a creamy off-white, was yellowing; it needed a new coat. And except for his framed diplomas far off to the right, the wall was bare. It could use something, a watercolor landscape or portrait in oils. He had never thought to put anything there or to ask what kind of art she did. Maybe she would make something for him, something to hang on that wall. He'd never had much time to learn about art, so maybe she could teach him everything. Maybe she would let him watch while she worked.

✿✿✿✿

When she appeared in his office a week later she seemed even more beautiful. She offered her hand in a manner at once formal and familiar. For a moment he stood speechless before her like a boy in awe of a schoolteacher he secretly loved. Never had he seen her so artfully made up, the lipstick and eye-shadow applied with a touch accenting the lines that once had defined her beauty in its maturest young bloom. When she let go of his hand and stood apart smiling at him, his eyes took her completely in. She was wearing a tight-fitting blue dress, and her neck and arms were brilliant with gems. But his eyes were merely distracted by them. Instead he saw her form, perfect and complete, a sculpture against the light of the window in front of which she stood. As he turned away from her to find a chair, the shadowed image of her stayed in his mind until he looked up again.

"How are you?" he asked as he eased himself down.

She moved her chair to her left, in position to face the wall. Then she sat, looked impassively at the wall, and folded her hands in her lap.

"You look very nice today."

"But I don't feel well," she replied in a quiet voice, not taking her eyes from the wall. "I think these tests are wearing me down. I don't think they're doing me any good. I want to go home. And that's what George thinks too, isn't it?"

For the first time he noticed the strands of grey in her hair, and then he saw the rough withering on the side of her neck. She crossed one leg over the other and let herself slump in her chair.

"And we think there's another lump in my neck."

32

He could see it too, as he had seen it hundreds of times before – the secret growth of the disease, the skin turning yellow, the slow withering away. She turned and looked at him.

"What's happening to me? Do you know? Tell me the truth. Can you really help me at all?"

The words came to him immediately, but he turned away from them. She should go home. She should go home with George and die in bed.

"I want you to tell me honestly what you think is best," she said, her voice cracking with helplessness.

Then he saw his chance. As he had done hundreds of times before he got up from his chair and walked over to her, and as she lowered her head he put his hand on her shoulder.

"I'm sorry," he said. "My diagnosis makes it clear that under the present circumstances your outlook is unfavorable."

"It's terminal?"

He nodded yes.

"How long?"

"About six months, at this rate."

She sank into her chair, running a finger over a strand of hair out of place. Then she sat up, smoothed down her dress, and looked out the window.

"So there's nothing you can do?"

"I wouldn't say that. There are certain treatments we can apply. They are demanding of your time and energy and we would have to begin them right away, but they might change your prospects considerably."

"How considerably?"

He walked through the corridors of his hospitals, stopping to look into rooms along the way. Here he saw eight months and there eleven or thirteen looking up hopelessly at him, and by the furthest stretch of imagination he saw two years. He was sixty-seven years old. An average man lived to be seventy-two.

"If you take your treatments seriously and let us take care of you the way we think is proper and right, we think we could add five years to your life."

&#10086;&#10086;&#10086;&#10086;

Before he finally agreed to let her go she collapsed into his arms and wept. Then suddenly she was gone, abandoning him without a word after his office door closed to the silence of corridors. For the first time she had fallen apart, her loss of composure showing itself as a blush of shame that blossomed in the face that she had so carefully prepared for even him to see. He saw it more clearly after she left the room. She was ashamed to see what her disease was doing to her dignity. Like some young girl contemplating herself naked in the mirror for the very first time, she had to look away. He was certain of one thing: From the moment he pronounced sentence on her she never looked at the wall, or spoke, or listened, to her George. Perhaps his sentence had finished off her George. If not, what was her George thinking when he saw her in her doctor's arms?

He could be a doctor no more that day. He canceled his appointments and left everything scattered on his desk. "Tell them the doctor's ill," he instructed the nurse.

At home he sat by the window looking out. He could not get over how disappointed he was with her embrace, how soft she was rather than firm, and how she seemed to slip like sand through his hands as she sat down again. More than anything he wanted more of her. For a moment he had her where he wanted her, but he had too easily let her slip away. Now if he failed to act he would lose her for good.

His hands were shaking as he dialed the number of her hotel, and when he asked for her by name the operator did not understand.

"No," he said again. "Strom. Mrs. Strom."

"One moment please."

His heart sank as he waited. What if she had already checked out?

"Yes? Hello?"

Her voice seemed distant and small.

"Adele?"

"Yes?"

"This is Dr. Willard."

Again he could not find words.

"Are you alone?"

"Yes."

"I'm very concerned about you. I don't think you should be alone at a time like this."

"That's very kind of you."

"I wonder... would you consent to allow me to see you at this time, or perhaps to accompany you to dinner later tonight?"

He heard the composure in her voice, the formality that was her way.

"Oh, you are too kind."

"I would like to put you at ease about the treatments we discussed."

"That won't be necessary, Dr. Willard. I'll be leaving in the morning for home. There's an idea I'm working on."

"Could I see you still this evening?"

"How charming and kind you really are," she replied. "But I don't think you understand. It just wouldn't work out. I've been happily married all my life."

He shaved and showered and put on his very best suit, and he called a cab to deliver him to his favorite restaurant. At the end of his meal he called for champagne. And he sat late looking at the faces surrounding him.

In his room that night he carefully removed his clothes and put them where they belonged. He found himself a bit giddy, standing naked beside his bed. How foolish of me, he thought, to try to keep her from going home. He should have known that something always has to be left behind, at least seventeen grams of soul. And the shame that she left behind in his office before she went away? Was that not perhaps really his shame? Never before had the truth about six months worth of living been stretched into a five-year lie.

He sat on the edge of the bed and looked again at his sixty-seven year-old arms, stomach, and legs, the sagging skeleton that was himself. Was he gaining too much weight? Glancing over his shoulder he saw that his wife was still holding her pose. He lifted first one and then the other leg into the bed, pulled the blanket over himself and turned on his side, facing her.

"Now tell me honestly," he said as he reached up to turn off the light, "what you really think."

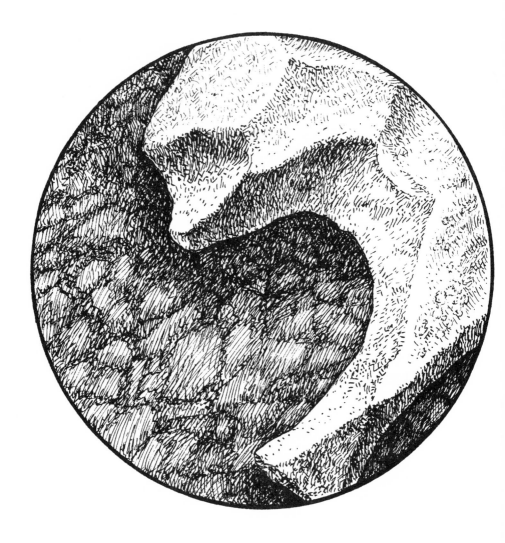

# THE TRIP AROUND THE MOON

In her eighty-seven years Hannah Greenleaf had seen her share of the wonders of the world. Suddenly men flew in the sky and walked in space, and they went so fast in their cars she got dizzy and had to sit down. She had seen Houdini and Mae West in the flesh, and once, right after she finished her college degree, had traveled the length of the Mississippi on the great Delta Queen. And nothing but her trip around the moon measured up to her honeymoon in Grand Canyon National Park.

The bad times were so strange that they too were hard to believe. In 1918 her younger brother was reported missing in the Black Forest, and in the next world war her only son disappeared in a submarine. Yet they were still present on the front porch of the house in which she had spent fifty-seven years of her life, there where she sat at the window waiting every morning for the mailman to arrive. After he carried her over the threshold when she was only eighteen, Frank was there too for all those years. And Frank was no mailman. She didn't wait for him every day the way she did for a few words from her brother or son or the daughter who moved away to three other states, leaving her alone in the long years of grief that seemed strangest to her. The sadness to which she surrendered every night in that house carried her away into grey mornings that stretched into decades as unclear as the faces she now saw every day in the hospital corridor. She was sure of it: It was the sadness that made her breathing so hard. Her only brother and only son. Imagine that. The daughter too, the very last one, who was born laughing out loud. The doctor himself said this girl had a special destiny, for he had never seen anyone laughing at the moment of birth.

When Marian, the nurse's aide, first appeared in Hannah's room, the old woman drew a sheet up to her face, her eyes following every move Marian made in the room. Blushing shyly as she went about her chores, Marian threw smiles over her shoulder until Hannah lowered her sheet.

"And what color are your eyes?" Hannah finally said.

"Hazel."

"And what's your name?"

"I'm Marian, your new aide."

Hannah leaned forward for a closer look. "That doesn't ring a bell. Are you sure?"

Marian smiled as she set the pillow behind Marian's back. "I've been called a lot of things recently, so you can call me what you want."

From then on Hannah lay in wait for her. When dinner was served Hannah refused her tray unless Marian delivered it to her. When the doctor came Marian had to be present to hold her hand. And the other nurses had no right to enter her room. "I had a daughter," Hannah told her after a week, "except I never see you laugh the way she did. What did you say her name was again?"

"My name is Marian."

"Oh yes, of course," Hannah replied. "But dear me, I can't imagine how old you are. How old did you say you were again?"

Marian, so suddenly no longer nineteen, had to think before she spoke. "I'm twenty-nine."

"My, my," Hannah said with a sad little shake of her head, "I imagine you'll tire of all my talk and be going off somewhere faraway soon."

Running from one patient to another left Marian little time to imagine how her time flew. She needed to change everything--soiled sheets, bedpans, bandages on festering sores – while hurrying to hold frightened hands in the middle of the night and press damp washcloths on feverish brows. When she got a moment she sat staring at a windowless wall, weariness suddenly weighing her down, the middle of the night as dim and vacant as the corridors of the hospital. Twenty-nine years old. Female. Employed four years. Nurse's aide. Minimum wage. Enough to pay for groceries, rent, car repairs. And required to smile when spoken to.

It was a Saturday, 4:30 a.m., when Hannah summoned her again.

"Would you take my arm, dear girl, while I go on a little stroll. I'm so very wide awake again, and there's nothing I need more than to get out for a bit of fresh air."

"Certainly," Marian said, "a little stroll, but no running today."

Hannah took small steps as she edged away from her bed, now and then pausing to look over her shoulder at Marian. By the time she reached the window the sun was beginning to appear on the horizon, its light like the glow of a city approached from distant country roads.

"Have you ever been to New York?" Hannah asked.

"Someday," Marian replied. "I made a friend promise he would take me there. Then Paris someday, of course."

"Ah, New York is one of the wonders of the world. From the sky the lights look like diamonds and jewels."

She led Marian away from the window, throwing one more glance over her shoulder at the rising sun. Hannah had trouble with the bathroom door, so Marian opened it for her. Hannah smiled before sitting on the toilet, unaware that her nightgown was clinging to her hips. Quickly Marian pulled it up out of the way and then stepped back, just outside the door.

Hannah sat hunched over a long minute as if slipping into sleep. Then she stirred and sat up straight.

"Frank never said yes or no."

"Did you call me?" Marian asked as she stuck her head inside the door.

Hannah had slumped down again, her eyes distant and glazed, her skin drooping from her small-boned frame as if she were a candle melting away.

"I can't remember your husband's name," Hannah said.

Marian smiled as she assisted her. "I'm not married," she said. "But I have a... boyfriend."

"A boyfriend or a lover?"

"Why Hannah Greenleaf, I'm surprised at you," Marian said with her smile.

Hannah grinned. "He's a lover, isn't he?"

She had shared the same apartment with him for over three years, and he did pay a third of the rent. But what at first seemed like love, the sure thing, had become something less. When she left for work at midnight, he was already asleep. When she returned she fell exhausted into bed, relieved to have it all to herself.

"You promise not to tell?"

"Promise," Hannah said.

"You're right. He's a lover."

Hannah reached for Marian's arm and pulled herself up.

"You know, Frank never did say yes or no. Don't you think he should have said yes or no?"

"Oh yes, of course," Marian chimed to humor her.

Hannah tugged at Marian's arm and led her to the window again. In the courtyard the bushes and trees were dark and still, but in the distance lights were visible in windows here and there. The lambent glow of the rising sun seemed soft against a streak of orange and blue reflecting off a billowing sea of low-lying clouds. Hannah stared at the scene without saying a word, her eyes distant and sad.

"Sometimes I'm just not sure I could survive another trip like that," she said.

"You needn't worry about anything," Marian said. "There's really nothing to worry about."

"Do you really think I could?"

Hannah stared off into the dawn again, suddenly unaware that her question required a response. In the courtyard a bird lifted itself from an old elm and streaked off, black against the sky.

"I promised you. Now can you promise me one little thing?"

"I think so," Marian said, letting go of Hannah's arm.

"We were on our vacation, Frank and I, and we were walking on the beach. That's when I saw him first – the stranger following me with his eyes. He was sitting on the sand and he had sunglasses on, and I could see that he was watching only me. You have to promise you won't tell a single soul."

"Promise."

"The next day I was alone on the Navy pier. There were boats everywhere, all of them grey except one, the one with the little blue flag. And it had a mast and lovely white sails. And there were numbers painted in blue on both sides, and a steering wheel made of brass and wood inside the cabin of the boat. I thought it was the most lovely of all the boats, because it was shiny and white and I could hear the wind singing in my ears as it rushed by.

"And when I turned my gaze away from the sea I found the stranger next to me. At first I thought he was a Naval man, but he was wearing a white dinner jacket with a carnation in the lapel. Oh my, I thought, he isn't wearing his sunglasses.

I got bold with him. "'Are you stopping for me?'

"'If you will kindly allow,' he replies.

"Now you know, my girl, that a stranger should not take liberties with a woman that way. One can never be too sure, especially in these troubled times.

"'Could I have the pleasure of your presence?' he says as he steps between me and the end of the pier.

"I was trembling all over, but I did manage some words. 'Is there some mistake? I am not who you think I am.'

"His next words swept me off my feet. 'I will require nothing immoral of you.'

"'Then what is it you want?'

"'Could I have the honor of your presence for a trip around the moon?'

"'A trip around the moon?' Well I had never given it much thought before. What with cars, airplanes, spaceships, I always thought of myself as an old-fashioned girl. I could hardly imagine such a thing.

"'You want me?'

"'Yes, you.'

"Well I was, as you can imagine, taken aback. 'How will we go?'

"He pointed to the boat.

"'Can I bring my husband along?'

"'I'd be delighted if he would accompany us,' was all he said.

"So I went back and told Frank all about this wonderful gentleman and his boat, how he was planning this trip. But Frank, knowing him, you see he didn't pay any mind to what I had to say. He asked me about the motor in back, how big it was. I told him I wasn't sure, didn't remember seeing it, but I explained about the cable running along the left side of the boat. Then I just came out with it: Do you want to go or not? And he never said yes or no. He was reading a newspaper and he never put it down. So I told him he'd better get some things together if he was expecting to come.

"My heart was pounding when I said those words, because I'm not someone who talks back. But I didn't eat my words, not a single one, and I felt better when I saw the gentleman waiting for me on the pier again. The sun had risen but the fog was still hanging over the water just twenty feet offshore. I remember the lazy way the waves kept coming in, calm and regular, and the clean cool air. I saw him standing by the boat. He had a white jacket on, but this time it was a Navy jacket and I saw the decorations on his chest. That's when I knew I didn't have anything to worry about. He held his hand out and helped me to a seat on the boat, then put a yellow and orange shawl over my shoulders. He was thirty-five or thirty-six, and he had shaved his face very smooth, and his eyes were brown, very dark."

"Was he a handsome man?" Marian asked.

Hannah tilted her head toward the window. "No," she finally concluded, "not especially. But he was something else. And I remember for sure the shawl on my shoulders because it was getting cold, and I knew I would need it once the wind began to blow. I was amazed at how smoothly we began. He pulled a string and the engine started right up. It made a low gurgling sound at first but then you could hardly hear it at all.

"'Will I have to be strapped down?' I asked.

"'I think not,' he says. 'There is some fear at first, but not if you keep your balance through the first stage of the trip.'

"He readjusted the shawl so it covered my left arm.

"'As we ascend you will feel as if you're falling. Don't tighten your hands into fists. Just open them, let them float free.'

"He smiled before lifting a thumb to signal that we were on our way. The engine was making a low sweet hum and before I knew it we were gliding away."

"What was it like?" Marian asked.

Hannah's eyes widened as they searched the sky beyond the most distant trees. "It was like nothing else. The first thing I saw was New York again, all those lights laid out like jewels in the dark. Did you like New York when you were there?"

Marian smiled. He, her lover, had been to New York, had bought her Paris perfume while there, real Paris perfume. She had tried a touch on her arm, the fragrance of strange flowers and flesh, then sealed the vial for a special night that never arrived.

"New York is incredible," Marian said.

"Yes," Hannah went on, "it was... slippery – the way we glided off, slid off the water into the air and from there we tilted and I could see, almost a hundred miles below, a green and brown patchwork quilt. The sun was already up, and there was a flock of geese flying V-shaped away. And only when I leaned the other way did I see that the moon was full, almost pure white. So we were in the middle of it all, the sun and moon rising on both sides."

"'This is beautiful,' I said to him, 'absolutely beautiful.'

"He just nods, but as he did I became aware of my hands. They were clenched tight, my knuckles white as bones.

"'Just let them go,' he whispers to me.

"They came open of their own free will. It was as if I had waved a wand, for suddenly we seemed to really take off, just slide away. Then I knew we were on the other side of the moon."

"How did you know?" Marian asked.

"The sun and moon were so beautiful, like nothing else. That's when I knew for sure."

Hannah let go of Marian's hand, turned from the window, and retreated to her bed. She paused at the edge of the bed, looking around the room as if she were a little girl lost in strange city streets.

"I remember these things. Going to the hospital. It was an easy labor, the easiest by far. She laughed and laughed. And I was laughing because the doctor... well the doctor must have been in a hurry because he had his pants halfway unzipped. Now that was the funniest thing, don't you think, even though I really wanted a boy."

She leaned back on her pillow, her eyes searching for the window again.

"You know how you forget what's up and what's down. All those stars and here we are just sliding along."

"Did the stranger say anything to you?"

"Yes," Hannah replied. "Don't think I would forget such a thing. He came right out with it too – asked me if I thought I was doing anything wrong."

"What could you have been doing wrong?"

"Because Frank was so many miles away by now. Because he never said yes or no. Because he never actually gave me permission to go."

"What did you say to him?"

Hannah's eyes darted away again. "For the first time in my life I didn't care what Frank said, and I didn't feel scared of it. He would have to take it or leave it, because on the other side of the moon it doesn't matter if what you do is right or wrong."

Marian sat on the edge of the bed and took Hannah's hand, its skin loose and thin, a brown cellophane covering small bones.

"Did the stranger say why he wanted to go on this trip?"

"Oh yes," Hannah replied. "We talked all night. He had been there many times before, but he never liked going alone."

"Why you?"

"Because I was a perfect stranger to him, that's why."

Hannah's eyes found the window again. "Ah Marian, I felt like laughing out loud. Then when Frank died I had the house all to myself. At first we were just sliding along and I was asking about the moon and he told me we couldn't see it quite yet. He adjusted my shawl again because I was getting cold. Not that I was afraid. I suppose I was just getting ahead of myself."

"And then you returned?"

"Yes, returned. It became harder to breathe, and I couldn't hold my breath any more. That's when I knew we were back."

She turned over on her side, away from Marian.

"He showed me the medals he won in the war. There were six of them, and I'll never forget his face, smooth as a boy's. And he had shined his shoes especially for me. He threw the rope over one of the posts on the pier and he told me not to worry about the boat. He took my hand and kissed it and I couldn't help looking back over my shoulder at him as I walked away. He was just standing there by that big beautiful boat. That's the way I see him now, just standing there with one hand in his pocket."

"And what was his name?"

Hannah turned toward Marian, a confused look on her face. Then she opened into a smile.

"Why, he never did ask my name."

"And what did Frank say?"

"Nothing at all. He gave me his usual stare. He had his feet up on the sofa and he never bothered taking his shoes off. And there were ashes from his pipe all over the floor and a half-empty coffee cup on the table next to him. It was twelve minutes after five when I walked in the door, and I didn't care how my hair looked, because it started raining and I got soaked through and through and I didn't care about anything any more."

Marian straightened the sheet and pulled the blanket over Hannah's shoulders again.

"Frank asked me, 'Where were you all night?' And all I said was 'Out. Just out.' And that's all I ever said to him ever again."

Marian caught a glimpse of herself in the mirror above the small sink across from Hannah's bed. For the third day in a row she had only slept five hours. She was tired again and again and again. Her white uniforms smelling of old age when she threw them in the wash. Her lover's dirty socks and underwear in the same water swirling back and forth. The light in the room that put a pale yellow cast on her skin, and the dark circles under both eyes. She would be home by eight-thirty this morning and today she would go immediately to sleep, and again she would sleep as long as she needed to sleep, even if it was dark when she awoke and again had to return in an hour to work.

Suddenly Hannah sat up in bed, her eyes wide and alarmed. "You have to promise me! You said you would! You can't breathe a word of this to a single soul! Not a word! You have to promise!"

Marian took Hannah's hand and stroked it until the old lady slipped down under the covers again. Within a minute Hannah's breathing calmed itself and she closed her eyes. Then Marian turned off the light over the mirror and quietly walked out. As she closed the door behind her she felt a quiver of sexual desire. She looked behind her, then began running her hands up and down the sides of her white dress and over her breasts. Suddenly she began to laugh as she glanced over her shoulder down the long empty corridor. "A trip around the moon," she said out loud. "I'm going to kick his ass out as soon as I get home." She laughed hysterically, her laughter echoing off the walls of the corridor as she walked away.

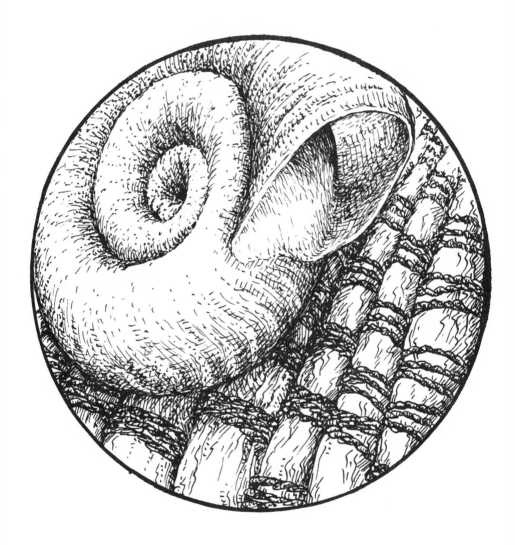

# A SYMMETRY

When I asked if I could return the favor somehow, his smile seemed to say equally no and yes. He had just stopped my hat from blowing away, had ventured in front of a car to step on it and was hastily trying to restore it to its original form. "Yes, a very nice hat. I hope it's not bent hopelessly out of shape."

Armand DuPère let me buy dinner but not the Bordeaux. "It's almost Christmas," he said, "so I have to have something to give." He had more to offer than I imagined from looking at him, his nervous hands and untidy hair, the face so pale and unfazed by the influence of wine. With the first glass we struck a common chord. Though I was old and young enough to be his only remaining son, we were both wary enough to know we were lonely men. Was I a widower too? "Yes, but after the divorce." And no, neither of us currently had a woman in his life.

What, then, did he do?

"Can you believe?" he said. "Physics – all my life."

He was nervously scrawling designs on the white tablecloth, strange shapes that curled in on themselves like the flowers on a paisley tie.

"What's all that?" I asked.

He looked up and smiled. "Chaos. The kind of physics I've been doing for the last sixteen years."

He tried to explain, but I had to interrupt. Physics, always impossible for me, was also too much a thing of the past. Could he draw me a plain and simple picture of what his work was all about?

"Do you know any calculus?" he asked.

"None."

He paused as if to test my desire to know, and I was afraid that all he would see was my loneliness. He smiled before leaping right into the middle of things. All matter was essentially chaotic, flying blindly over the heads of the millions who spent their hours in factories and shopping malls. He began scrawling more shapes on the tablecloth, his words outracing his hands, and within moments everything was mainly nonsense to me.

"I'm afraid," I said, "that I'm not equal to it. Could you try another picture? Something simple for a dull ape like me."

"Look at it like this," he said. "God was the Great Geometer, the perfectly whole mind, all symmetry, both He and She at once. Then once upon a time – in the beginning, let's say – there was a gigantic skyburst, like a huge blossoming firework. What we call the Big Bang. And what we call space and time were suddenly filled with God's mind, everything spreading, fizzling out. Are you following me so far?"

That much I could see clearly enough through his eyes. They widened as he was telling it, as if the picture, emerging from a dark space in the back of his mind, was an event he was experiencing for the very first time.

"Yes," I said, "I see."

But we needed a little more time. "Perhaps another dinner and bottle of wine," he offered. "Another little talk like this at Mamma Lucia's again."

His hair was greyed but never turned white, and the quiver in his hand grew more unsteady as the weeks disappeared into months, a palsy also eventually taking possession of his knees. When winter came around again I had to be especially careful not to let go as he took baby steps across the ice and snow toward the door of Mamma Lucia's and the small table for two next to the window magically distancing us from the slur of traffic outside.

And he kept trying to explain how everything went.

"What happened after that first blossoming is all history. A sort of petering out."

"Yes, like those starburst fireworks that dissolve the moment they begin to nose-dive toward the ground."

"It's the Higgs Field, full of Higgs particles. Do the particles exist?" He lowered his voice and leaned in close to me. "I'm absolutely convinced they do."

A Higgs particle? How in the world was I supposed to know?

"I remember," I broke in, "the fireworks we had every Fourth of July. Everybody came out to watch, and I used to get as close as I could to the men who shot them up. We thought it was wonderful stuff and we even brought our radios. There was a local radio announcer, Tommy Thorp, who used to give a play-by-play description of each rocket going off, and then we mainly waited for the grand finale, when someone would light a fuse and a whole bunch would go off all at once."

48

DuPère smiled his usual sad smile. "And everybody cheered, thought it was grand."

"Yes."

"And then what? A little sadness set in – everyone walking quietly home. Everything suddenly over and done."

"Not for me," I replied. "I couldn't wait for the next day. I'd get up before breakfast and run to the park and start looking for all the little fragments of the fireworks – scraps of paper, little leftover parts of tubes, bits of powder that weren't burned up. We used to scrape them into a coffee can and take the can to somebody's garage."

"And stick matches to it," DuPère said.

"Yes, blow things up – tin cans, piles of little twigs, anthills. Weren't we bad little beasts in those days?"

"Yes," DuPère said as his hand made a display of his bent body, "and look at us now."

If in the instant of the Big Bang the universe had perfect symmetry, the symmetry began to dissipate in the very next billionth of a millisecond, the perfection of the starburst immediately fading. And in time everything began going off-center, equators bulging, galaxies flinging out spiral arms, clustering into massive globs near the edges of space, space itself curving in on itself like a snake with its tail in its mouth, undulating as it struggled to swallow itself. And here we were too, old men curling in on ourselves like drying weeds.

"You're beginning to see it," DuPère said.

And suddenly it was a Saturday night again. I was alone in my apartment and it was already five-sixteen. I won't say he came to mind immediately, for he had been there, vaguely off and on, from that time he had handed my hat back to me. Was it too late to call him for dinner again? He had been beginning to insist on eating precisely at six. If I called immediately and the traffic had mercy on us, we could make it with a minute to spare. The alternative was to spend the night with a book. My loneliness was all there, big as a shadow lengthening out before me as I walked faster down some deserted street, especially now that he was visibly weaker, his steps more uncertain, his skin tighter over the veins and bones of his hands, even his hair thinning, falling out in clumps. A dread I could not face sent a shiver through me. I reached for a book and opened it. As I held it in my hand one of the down pages furled up and turned over on its back, coming gently to rest on the facing side. I actually felt the small breeze the page made as it turned, and a chill ran up my spine. I rushed to the phone. "Oh God," I said as I dialed, "I hope it's not too late."

"I'm so glad you called," he said as I led him into Mamma Lucia's again. "It was one of those nights – you know, that could have gone here or there or nowhere at all. And I'm so glad it ended up here... "

"With you," I added to save him from using the words that would have made me blush.

Was it that night he could not keep himself still – kept developing an equation on the tablecloth? I stopped him before he got to an equal sign. If all had devolved from original Symmetry, the Great Geometer's Mind, how did he account for the persistence of symmetries?

"Symmetries? For example?" he asked.

"For example, salamanders."

"Ah yes, salamanders. They are tidy little beasts, aren't they, when they lie straight and still."

"And, for example, all naturally occurring spheres... raindrops, planets, moons." To show him I had done some homework too: "And there are certain crystals which have lattice symmetries, and the methane molecule is a perfect tetrahedron. And look at all those fish swimming in schools."

"And ladybugs."

"And the great animals – tigers and man – all bilaterally symmetrical."

He laughed. "Yes, all but the innards. A mess in there. The liver, the heart – so much off-center inside."

"Maybe we should thank your Great Geometer for that," I said. "Maybe his way of getting us through our dull routines."

DuPère smiled shyly and looked away. "Like both of us being alone tonight instead of here. We wouldn't be having our little fling."

He let me help him up the stairs to his apartment that night, and asked for my help in getting him to bed. I left him sitting there, the lines on his face looking more tired than ever before but his eyes full of an abstract intensity gazing beyond me or any object in the room. I abandoned him in his silence without saying good-night, convinced that he was chasing another equation into one of the dark corners of his mind. It was then I realized that he had only a few more months, maybe weeks, to live.

Everything had to be accomplished at once. When we met again he tried again to get me looking at the galaxies. Here we were again – another winter night in Mamma Lucia's. Out there the universe was aging too, and some stars, perhaps whole seas of them, were already dead, our light-year distance from their deaths making us the beneficiaries of their subtle brilliances. What then when their deaths caught up with us, all those lights going out? No need to worry, DuPère laughed, for our deaths would catch up with their subtle brilliances first.

He had developed some incontinence and had to make frequent stops. The systems weren't working right, yet everything seemed stuck on go. Like the traffic in the streets, the crime that horrified us both, the cities swelling with misery, the rivers, lakes, now oceans filling with filth. "And I forget to flush," he muttered to himself as he returned to his chair.

"Well, then, what about it," I said, "the symmetry? How come there's so much of it all around?"

He chuckled as he doodled on the tablecloth. "Maybe because the Old Geometer is nostalgic about a former way of life, can't help slipping into it now and then – maybe can't keep himself from returning to infant ways."

He seemed to remember everything from his youth. He was only six when he first laid eyes on Diane. She had long blond hair and very blue eyes, and he followed her home from school. This went on for three whole years. Then he was at a birthday party and everyone was playing a game, Truth or Consequences, when he stood up and told the Truth. Yes, he loved Diane. Diane put her hands over her face, screamed, and ran out of the room. He was mortified, humiliated, undone. He cried all the way home, but he couldn't keep himself from loving her. He kept looking everywhere for a glimpse of her long blond hair and very blue eyes – and he kept following her home from school every day.

"Did you end up marrying her?"

"No, I married a wonderful brunette. But I kept seeing Diane everywhere – streets, movies, store windows, everywhere. I couldn't get over her."

I tapped my head. "Your interest in chaos came from her."

"No, the music came first, because I guess I was naturally good at it. They sat me down at a piano and I played chords, things that sounded right. Everyone was amazed, but the lessons were a drag. I began seeing the notes on the page. Here they were – black and white little critters running up and down and all around, whole armies of them with their little flags, now and then one of them a Buddha Humpty-Dumpty just sitting there, brooding about the whole fuss, trying to make up his mind, thinking of ways to stay on that fence without falling off. The next thing I knew I began seeing numbers instead of notes. And then numbers everywhere I looked."

"But if everything's an equation, then this inclination toward symmetry that we've been talking about, order... "

"The coming fascist state," he whispered as he leaned in close. "The desire to achieve some abstract idea of perfection."

Yes, we agreed it was in both of us. But it was "out there" too – in the stars, in the very nature of things. The salamanders were its living sediment, and so were my raindrops and methane molecules, the circle and square, the isosceles triangle, pyramids, parthenons, sphinxes, sphincters. All naturally occurring in the radiant fallout of the universe, its enormous masses still alive with the power to mass-produce ancient tidy forms, this power visible in the eyes of salamanders staring back at us.

A chill went up and down my spine as I began seeing what DuPère's theory was all about. He felt my awe immediately, and suddenly we had nothing more to say to each other that night.

I called the next day and waited while the phone rang and rang. Finally he said hello. How was he today? "Actually," he said, "I'm somewhat out of sorts. A bit of the flu, it seems. And you?"

I had caught a cold.

"How did you catch it," he laughed, "in your arms?"

It had to be the other night, in Mamma Lucia's. Something there. Some little vermin on some doorknob, on some knife or fork. Something in the air. I remembered him sitting at the table across from me, an old man shriveling, dying, diseased. Repulsive. "I suppose I could have caught whatever I caught with a butterfly net, but I didn't think to bring one along. Maybe I brushed against somebody, so come to think of it maybe I did use my arms."

"And maybe you caught something bigger than a cold – a bit of my flu. Maybe you should see a doctor."

"You're a doctor."

"Only physics here. I'm not a real doctor."

"You're doctor enough for me. Maybe I talked too much when you called the other night with all that stuff about the Higgs Field. Maybe I should learn when to keep my mouth shut from now on."

Exactly when we talked on the phone or what we said I didn't recall. After we hung up our silence was an absence too, a blank dizziness like what I fell in whenever I tried to remember some little event, the meaning of some suddenly absurd word, some fact or face obstinately indifferent to revealing itself. As I was slipping toward sleep that night I turned in the wheel of memory, seeing myself as a boy standing alone in a field with a baseball in my hand. There was a little chill in the air, the first warm breath of spring, and I was the pitcher beginning that slow windup again, the curling in of arms and legs before the rearing back turns into the unfurling of boy out of himself. In front of me, cowering a bit under spindly legs, there I was too standing over home plate, my baseball cap askew, a little too big on my head.

"Well," I said when we met again at Mamma Lucia's the following night, "do you still have the flu? What did the doctor say?"

"A touch of the Asian flu. But nothing to worry about any more."

I listened while he explained. No doubt it was business as usual in some place near Bangkok, Rangoon, or Saigon. Then there was a flutter, quiver, some small spasm in the air, some slug waking up in the morning sun, extending its horns to get the feel of things. A bee brushing a flower-petal, breaking it from its stem. Or a butterfly extending a wing to veer left or right, then beating madly to get on course again toward some impossible Aztec mountainside. An invisible innuendo, misty connotation, transparent stir of air moiling up out of some steamy valley floor, the stir then overwhelmed, carried away by a current swept slightly askew by a moil of new air, then sucked in – and the rest is history: The current sweeps upward to hitch a ride from passing winds for its jet-stream passage to America where it descends and slows, picking up gravity in the dense carbon over crowded city streets, moiling again as it drifts down through cold skies as snow outside the window of Mamma Lucia's on a Saturday night.

"You caught your flu-bug virus that way?"

"See, not in a butterfly net," DuPère replied. "But I suspect that the person I brushed against ended up here that way. The snow. He took one look out the window at the snow and said, 'What a lovely night to have dinner at Mamma Lucia's again.' And here we all are that night."

I told him about my dream, how I was alone on a vast green field, winding up to throw the ball, how there I was also standing there with the bat in my hand, trying to hit the ball.

"What happened?" he asked.

"I'm not sure. There I was, saying to myself, 'Now watch the ball, don't take your eye from it.' And I saw it all the way, its seams spinning a little off-center, and something in me said yes, now, and I pulled the trigger with the bat."

"You blasted the ball over the fence and all the girls cheered."

"No, there was no fence. At the last second the ball fluttered, dipped away, and skipped along the ground. I never saw it again. I missed it by a mile. I whiffed, and one of the girls in particular laughed."

"Let her laugh," DuPère said as he smiled. "Africa desperately needs water these days. You may have caused a rainstorm in some God-forsaken place. Or a little Himalayan avalanche. Either way, it's okay. You did what you could."

"I know the kid who threw the ball was happy enough. I can still see that smug self-satisfied look on his face."

Three days later I tried him again, this time appearing unannounced at his door. I let myself in to find him alone in bed, turned away toward the grey window light. He did not stir as I approached, but I could see that he was alert, had been staring at the traffic below.

"How are you today?" I asked to break the silence in the room.

"Rather amazed," he replied as he struggled to sit up, "at the acceleration of the process."

"You feel worse?"

"I feel... increasingly out of sorts. Especially when I see what's happening out there."

The crime, the misery, the homelessness and alienation, the dog-eat-dog economics, the culture of distraction and greed. DuPère had a social conscience that kept him from magnifying his distress into a significance beyond what it merely was, particular and natural.

"Everything seems to be falling apart," I offered.

"Yes, widgets," he replied as he turned an agitated face toward me, "more and more of them everywhere you look. Toy blocks, cement blocks, whole blocks of city streets going on and on right out of sight. They're taking over the world. Pretty soon there will be nothing left of trees, swamps, woods."

"A sort of petering out."

"Of everything but widgets, all of them mass-produced."

"The end of nature."

He managed one of those sad smiles I had coming to me whenever I said anything too smart, at odds with one of the theories his lifetime of study had converted into fact. He lifted his nightshirt and ran his hand along the lower part of his back. "Now there's a goddamned pain here too."

I prepared a moist hot towel and held it in place, removing it every few moments to massage the area with my palms.

"No," he said as he twisted his neck back to get a look at me, "not the end of nature. The end of landscapes, yes – streams with clear water in them, prairie fields, forests, even fresh air. But the cars rolling off the assembly lines, the coffee cans, sticks of chewing gum, best-selling books, plywood sheets, and eight-penny nails – they're the new natural order of things, the natural process fulfilling itself."

"Widgets – all heading where?"

He smiled again. "The end of chaos – where else? A dull little one-room apartment, like everyone else. With a little parking place outside."

⚜⚜⚜⚜

The conclusion came a few weeks later, and I was the only one privileged to be in the room as it was making itself known. I found myself on my way to him again, this time on a dreary December evening lit up by Christmas lights hung on trees. I must have been looking at them instead of the thin sleet icing the sidewalks and streets. I lost my balance and slipped to one knee, god-damning my carelessness as I got up and pushed on.

I was still brushing myself off as I stood in front of his bed. "I fell," I said.

"You just fizzled, took a little nose-dive," he mumbled without turning my way, his voice muffled in the pillow from which he had not lifted his head.

"Yes."

"You whiffed. And everybody cheered, thought it was grand."

"Yes."

"And one of the girls in particular laughed."

"The one I really wanted and never got."

Throughout his ordeal he had sustained the composure and intensity of his extraordinary intellect, his eyes steady and determined to chase down any strange new equation teasing him. It usually did not take long for me to remind myself that for him things were, well, numbered, but not in any easy way like dollars, dozens of eggs, or days. On this particular occasion I could sense that he was far from his former self. He was cowering, his knees pulled up tight into his chest, and shivering beneath thick blankets in an overheated room oppressed by a foul odor drifting about. When finally he lifted his head I could see that he was virtually unable to open his eyes, let alone willing to search the room for things, relations, to figure and calculate.

"There, there," I said as I sat on the bed and began stroking his hair.

He let out a deep breath as he struggled to find words. "I'm beside myself, utterly ... " He lifted his head. "What day is it?"

"December 18."

"Ah yes. The Old Geometer came down to earth a week from now."

"Yes, and I've got a present for you."

"And here we are."

Wearied by his effort to speak, he let his head sink into the pillow again. And as I sank down with him he made space for me on the bed, enough for me to stretch my legs out, lie down close to him and throw my arm over his back. I felt the slow rise and fall of his chest, and several times as I slipped toward sleep I awoke with a start, terrified that the breathing had stopped. But he was still there, his breaths slow and regular, uninterrupted by the strokes I was giving him with my hand. When I awoke it was completely dark outside and in the room, but he was sitting up looking down at me.

"Are you feeling okay?" he asked.

"The nap did me good."

"Sorry I'm not your beautiful woman."

"I'm sorry too," I said.

He lay down and moved his thigh in tight next to mine. The odor in the room drifted by again, so I turned away toward the small draft seeping through the window sill. With the fresh air came the noise of the streets, car horns, squealing tires, busses rumbling past. I closed my eyes and found myself in a white hospital room. Ah, what a beautiful girl, somebody said.

"Is this your hat?" DuPère whispered in his sleep.

"I hope it's not bent hopelessly out of shape. What's it like?"

He coughed a little as he tried to lift his head. "Oh?" he said tonelessly, indifferently, "it's very nice. Like nothing at all. With everything coming out equal for everyone. Any way you turn it, it all looks the same."

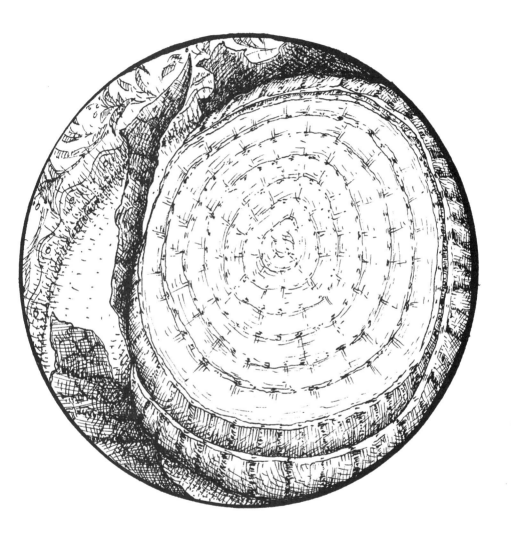

# OUTWARD AND VISIBLE SIGNS

The absurdity of Benny's death reduced us to wordlessness. All his words suddenly gone. In his last three hours he was running a marathon, he who used to stride so easily with words, pausing now and then to make a low humming sound, *ummm*, deep in his throat and chest. We knew he was finished when he broke into a sprint, his breaths too swiftly carrying him away, a few words now and then stumbling forward, as if afraid they would be left behind. We tried to slow him down even as we watched him outdistance us, diminishing into a dot. And when finally he held his breath one last time, we too, exhausted, gave up his ghost.

Afterward in my car I noted the event in the little notebook I kept for recording mileage: "Benny. January 26, 4:37 p.m."

Cancer of the brain. Benny, the encyclopedic mind. He who could recite long poems from memory, who had thought deeply about religion, literature, art, history and politics, friend always inspired into the night by truth shining in a glass of good wine. What a mind, we all agreed. What a brain.

We all misread the disease. "There are times," he wrote at the onset, "when I must be going too fast. My thinking seems to twist and turn, and the rest of me gets left behind in the dark. There I am, a little boy lost in my own house, seeing everything for the very first time. And everything strangely adding up."

In the Sixties he had been known to experiment with the varieties of religious experience. He had tried LSD and, just once, peyote. "After I had some of that stuff," he confided to me, "I felt as if I were walking in space. I was floating in a kind of nothingness and looking around full of amazement at how colorful the earth and moon and stars really were. There was no up or down or forward or back. And no fear. There I was, somewhere inside a big balloon suit, looking out past myself at a world where everything was free, afloat. And there was no fear."

He felt the fear when he came back to earth. "That was crazy," he said. "Why did I ever do that?" And twenty years later, looking back at himself, he managed to put everything into a normal perspective that let me down: "Those were crazy times. Now I'm glad to have my feet on the ground."

Toward the end, when the mysterious symptoms had him in their grip, nothing terrified him more than the thought he was going insane. His weird sensations were something else. "I'm sitting here reading philosophy," he wrote in a letter to me, "and suddenly the words make no sense. Not that they go blank as things would if we turned a page to find no more words. It's that the words turn into something else, shapes and colors that slowly turn – like a man in a tree, and a setting sun. And there's no pain or fear. No fear at all until I realize again that here I am – and suddenly the words on the page begin making sense again."

A few months before his doctor sentenced him we spent our evenings strolling along the river silently agreeing to agree, the silence summing up all the smart nonsense that had passed between us for years. Then we sat on the porch staring out at the night. "It's maddening how I feel when these moods come over me," he said. "In the car I'm driving along and suddenly I'm lost. It's wild and strange and wonderful until people start staring, yelling, honking their horns. Then I'm terrified – and what scares me most is that they'll think I'm crazy and won't let me in my own house."

Later, when Julie, his wife, called to tell me he was failing fast, she consoled both of us. "Well, at least he doesn't think he's crazy any more," she said, abruptly hanging up.

Even before he died I began missing the talk – all the words, full of light and heat and foolishness, turned this way and that, then inside-out until they brought us around to each other's point of view. *"Ummm,"* he would say as our wine gave out and our words gave us nowhere new to go, "let's call it a night."

Later, when I touched his arm as he lay on the hospital bed, his skin seemed like a membrane too thin to contain the small bones within. I drew immediately away, as if I would catch his disease.

Julie wrote me soon after he died: "Some days are harder than others. Peter, always the faithful son, came in from Toledo this weekend. He has Benny's eyes even though he's fair like me. I can't stop looking at him. It's wonderful, as if I'm seeing Benny alive in the flesh. But it's a haunted feeling. As if there's a ghost in the house, trapped inside another person. And I can't get to him. Peter has his own personality. I've always been very close to him, but I never expected him to start shouting Benny things. Now I can't stop looking at Pete. That look of vulnerability is there, only it's a new lifetime, a new script. I'm terribly glad, but at the same time I want to shake him and yell, 'Benny! Come out! Come out!' I keep waiting for something new, some new disaster, some new irony to take hold and bite, Benny to reappear, but so far things have been flat – day after day."

Nothing came out equal or fair, and nothing added up. She was closer to Benny than anyone, had a connection I couldn't approach. I put the letter in one of our favorite books.

᪥᪥᪥᪥᪥

I met Karl at a mountain resort about two months after Benny's death, my week there imagined as a way of warding off the late-winter blues. The resort would be far enough away to jar old habits, the mountain air in the region said to be rarer and warmer than that on the Great Plains where I lived. The brochure promised me afternoons on sunny mountain trails, evenings in front of the great fire with strangers looking for romance. Mornings I would spend as usual with a book.

When I finally arrived I still had the bitterness I had picked up along the way. Daily life is normally sour enough, but mine had been made acrid by the cancer that had singled out Benny's brain as if it were a delicacy on which the cancer could secretly feed until there was nothing left but the gorged self-satisfied disease. When reading the news or driving through city streets one saw too much violence and pain. Once on the road away from home I found the bitterness lengthening out so far in front of me that I could find no end to it in the overcast sky. There I was, driving through two days and evenings of dull grey matter, doing nothing better with my life than trying to get away. What really did I have to look forward to? At night I looked at the stars and sky as humans do, in awe of their beauty and contemptuous of their meaninglessness.

My first sight of the lodge did little to lighten my mood. While the mountains on all sides were massive and dark, the resort itself seemed fragile and askew, its cedar siding worn, the large fir posts supporting its broad deck leaning every which way. Against the broad grey rock of the mountainside on which it was perched, it seemed like a model made of sticks. Given the mountain streams flowing down on both sides, I concluded it would only be a matter of time before the lodge was swept away.

The interior was properly rustic, cozy enough for the eight of us scheduled to spend our time together there: Three couples – the

Bronsons, on a second honeymoon, Jim and Carolyn, not clever at hiding the fact that they were having an affair, and the Nortons, middle-aged and sullenly bigoted. I was the odd seventh to arrive.

Karl arrived last.

He was short, slight, and round-faced, his hair silvery and too long, his eyes moving nervously around the room, and his smile tentative and weak. But what arrested me immediately, even before I first saw him standing in front of the fireplace, was the sound in the room, Benny's sound, the unmistakable *ummm* that left me bewildered about where I was.

Karl walked up to me, his hand extended.

"Hi, I'm Karl Slater," he said, his smile blossoming. "Karl with a 'K'."

I asked him what he did.

"I'm a little burned out with lawyering," he replied, turning his head shyly away. "All that arguing back and forth. *Ummm.* I can't stand it sometimes, if you know what I mean. That's why I'm here. A little peace and quiet, you know. Have you met everyone else?"

"Yes," I said as I glanced at the dark end of the room.

"So when's your birthday?" he asked out of the blue.

"My birthday? Are you interested in astrology?"

"Not really. I don't know a thing about that. It's just, *ummm,* you have to start somewhere, you know."

"April 16. Forty-one."

"Interesting," he said as he took a seat by the fireplace. "Because mine's August 16, and I'm fifty-seven."

ও⋅ও⋅ও⋅ও

Long after the others drifted away to their rooms, Karl and I sat watching the embers in the fireplace losing their glow. We were content in our separate silences, now and then glancing up the way strangers do when they're attracted to each other but too shy to speak. There was something odd about the man, some alluring quality that made him seem extraordinary, or rather out of touch. More than once he caught me in the act of sizing him up, and each time he gave me a small smile, lowered his eyes and turned away. I thought of how Benny would have loved this room, the fire, the rough-hewn beams, how he would have been filling it with his wonderful talk and how, a bit dizzied by the wine in our words, we, satisfied, would have made our way to our separate rooms at the end of the night.

62

Karl suddenly looked up. "You're divorced."

I nodded. "You too?"

"Same as you," he replied. "Ten years now."

Ten years? I saw Erin, my ex-wife, as if I had never laid eyes on her before. Then she was gone, the way I couldn't conjure her face when I garnered the courage to announce to Benny and Julie that she and I were estranged. It seemed like yesterday and forever ago at once. Had a decade really passed? I did some quick figuring in my mind.

"Why did you assume ten years?"

"I figured it," he replied.

"A hunch?"

"No, *ummm*... I figured it, like I said. You – April 16, 1941, right? Me – August 16. You add forty-one and sixteen. That makes me fifty-seven. And you're forty-seven now, right? I was divorced ten years ago. Fifty-seven minus forty-seven is... "

"Ten."

"So I figured you were divorced ten years ago."

"Your logic is rather odd," I laughed.

"But it works," Karl said as he leaned toward me. "It always works. I can explain."

I stood to escape a sudden intensity in his eyes. "Maybe some other time. Right now I need some sleep."

శ్రీశ్రీశ్రీశ్రీ

It became clear rather immediately that the Nortons did not like Jim and Caroline. The young couple had let loose some stray comment that arched its back and hissed when Peter Norton picked it up. Gracie Norton turned up her nose whenever Jim and Caroline wandered by, but Peter set his mind on revenge.

"What did you say your last name was?" Norton asked Caroline, knowing she had a tendency to squirm when pressed for details.

"Wilson."

"Wilson?" Norton turned the name every which way in front of his eyes so that she would see him examining it. "Such an ordinary name. How could I possibly get it wrong? And you've been married how long?"

"Seven years," Caroline replied, her voice cracking a bit.

"Now isn't that nice," Norton said, turning first to the Bronsons, then to his wife. "Seven long years. And you two look like you're on your honeymoon. Seven long years of marital bliss."

"It's quite obvious," Norton announced to the rest of us the moment Caroline turned her back. "They're having an affair."

"And they're both still wearing wedding bands," Gracie chimed.

I hesitated too long, losing my chance to say it was none of my affair. For Karl stepped forward to be heard.

"Given... *ummm*... what we know, I don't think we can claim that theirs is an illicit love."

"I don't really care what they do with their time," Norton shot back. "I was just making a point."

Karl went nose-to-nose with him. "Your point would not stand in a court of law."

"Well," I whispered to Karl afterward, "they obviously are having a little *rendezvous*. It's written all over their faces, their little gestures. Not that I really care... "

"We'll have to see... "

"With our own two eyes, I suppose."

"More evidence will inevitably turn up without us snooping on them."

I tried making my joke again. "What kind of evidence would you like to see?"

"All we have is a few sevens so far," Karl said, arching his brow.

"Sevens?"

"The seven-year marriage, their room number here – thirty-four. And there are two sevens on the license plate of their car. I checked on that."

"Those sevens are supposed to prove their innocence?"

"I agree, they don't," Karl said. "There are too many missing links."

I blurted out a skeptical laugh. "More sevens? How many sevens would we need?"

"Maybe not sevens," he said, fixing his eyes on mine. "Maybe some other combination. You... *ummm*... just have to keep an eye out. You never know what you're going to get."

He turned shyly away, but I would not let him escape. "Why did you stick up for them earlier today?"

Karl smiled weakly as he edged toward the door. "Because Jim and Caroline are so obviously in love."

෨෮෨෮

Later that night by the fireplace I slowly eased my chair closer to Karl's.

"My theory," he began with a small exasperated shake of his head. "... *ummm*... I can't explain it, I'm not good with words, and maybe that's why, really, the lawyering doesn't sit well with me, if you know what I mean."

He sank into his chair as if he were surrendering himself to a distant past, and as he seemed to diminish in size before my eyes his voice grew more calm and confident, less frequently interrupted by Benny's hum.

"I was sick of everything," he said, "especially the lawyering, and I was becoming a little wreck of a man. Then one night – it was March 11 – I was alone in the living room. I happened to look at the coffee table, a magazine on top. I opened it at random to page thirty-four. It showed the picture of some battle scene from the Korean War, some rocky hillside being shelled by artillery. You could see places where men might be hunkered down, and in the lower middle there was some sort of small house with smoke billowing out. Everything in black and white, everything so clear, the snow, the cold, that terrible smoke, those small places where men were hiding in holes, freezing and terrified, the wounded screaming for help but nobody hearing because of the shells exploding all around. And I had music on the record player. A symphony. It was a little insane, the music and artillery all at once, and suddenly I was afraid, terrified, looking for somewhere to hide.

"They were all killed – everyone in the platoon except three. There was a group picture on the opposite page, with the faces of the three survivors circled. I looked at all three very carefully before I zeroed in on another face. He was in the second row, a little shorter than everyone else, and he had a sort of sad half-smile on his face. Though I couldn't quite place him anywhere in my memory, he looked oddly familiar to me, so familiar I couldn't take my eyes away. I found his name beneath the photograph. Terrance Karl. Karl. My name.

"Suddenly I wasn't afraid any more. Because he seemed content enough just the way he was, the sad half-smile on his face, the way he just kept looking calmly out – not directly at me, but out there just past my eyes. As if... *ummm*... everything would be all right, not to worry any more. Did you ever look at a photograph, especially an old black-and-white, how everything seems just there in it, once and for all? So that's how I felt, as if I was in the photograph and somebody else was looking at me.

"There was a sense of enormous relief. The shelling disappeared. All that was left was the music in the room, and it seemed to swell like ocean waves, a triumphant hymn over barbarity requiring me to go, follow it. I began dancing there all by myself, every part of me laughing, light and alive even after the music stopped. Later when I tried to explain, no words came. My wife kept asking me... *ummm*... what was wrong and I couldn't even get the word 'Nothing' out to her. All I could think of was that face in the photograph.

"The mood lasted several days, and I could bring it on by just looking at him in the photograph. Every day seemed bright and new. Little things seemed bizarre – a coffee cup, pen and paper, the clock on the wall, all little miracles. I couldn't help thinking about it more and more. The connection between me and the face in the photograph – if maybe the name Karl was just a coincidence. Then I realized one other thing: The music was a Carl Nielsen symphony. So suddenly there were three of us."

He leaned forward in his chair. "Are you beginning to see?"

"I'm beginning to see," I replied, "but that doesn't mean I don't fail to believe."

He chuckled a bit and looked shyly away. "It's not just a theory somewhere between Evolution and the idea that there are little green men living somewhere else in the galaxy. I'm talking about something *real*."

"Then it should be easy to explain logically."

"I really don't know how. It's just... *ummm*... when you start looking everything fits."

"Fits what?"

"For example, did you know it was Carl Nielsen's *Fourth* Symphony? The fourth of five. And I'm the fourth of five children in my family."

"So what?"

"And that symphony was finished in 1916."

"So what?"

"That's the year my father was born."

"Another coincidence."

"And his name was also Karl."

"So now we have four Karls."

"And Carl Nielsen died in 1931."

"As we all must."

"That's the year I was born."

I got up from my chair. "This is all very interesting, but I'd really better turn in for the night."

He rose to meet me, unaware that he was blocking my way to the door.

"I... *ummm*... you know. There's more, you know... evidences. Like 1865, the date of Nielsen's birth, and Slater, my last name, and the movements of the symphony, how... "

"Yes, of course, but I have to get some sleep."

"Yes, yes, you do look tired and depressed. But if you don't mind my asking you one little thing. Why is it you're here so alone?"

"So alone? Because my best friend just died, that's why. My very best friend."

"Ah yes, I figured that. Please let me know if I can help."

ᏆᏛᏆᏛᏆᏛᏆᏛ

My heart was still pounding when I crawled into bed. Who did he think he was? So alone. Benny, his face, his voice, everything gone, and I, his very best friend, abandoned to this little wreck of a man named Karl and his little evidences. Like 1865, the date of Nielsen's birth, and Slater, Karl's last name, and the movements of the symphony. What a little fool he was, not to make anything of the fact that Nielsen's name was spelled with a "C".

I kept hearing everything the Nortons said.

"I swear I know you from somewhere," Peter Norton said to Caroline as he sized her up.

"I think I told you before," she replied. "I'm from Detroit."

Mrs. Norton arched her brow. "Our daughter Sylvia is from Detroit."

"Is she still there?"

"Of course not, you little charm. How would you like it having colored people dealing drugs in your neighborhood? Besides, she's always been faithful to her man."

"Maybe you know her," Peter Norton said. "She used to live on Tireman Boulevard."

"Is she a Wilkerson?" Caroline asked.

"Why yes," Mrs. Norton replied, seeing clearly now who Caroline's real husband was. "Do you know Sylvia Wilkerson?"

Caroline's face fell as streaks of pink appeared on her neck. "No."

And I saw Peter Norton smirk as Caroline tried to squirm past him toward the door.

"Still," Karl was saying to them all, "there's good reason to believe we can work all these problems out. The crime, the wars, the black versus white."

"Very remarkable ideas," Norton broke in, his voice drawing blood with its sarcastic edge. "And to think you're a lawyer too."

"My own wife cheated on me," Karl was saying, "but what's the real difference between a kiss and a pinch? It was at a square dance one November night. The man with the fiddle said change partners, so I gave her a twirl and away she went into another man's arms. And they're still married to this day. Now isn't that nice?"

Then I played the hero's role, rushing into their midst, turning a new bottle of wine in the light.

"So let's drink to all lovers here tonight," I said as I lifted my glass to Karl. "Let no one come between those whom love has joined together here!"

As the Nortons turned tail and slithered away I slipped out from beneath my pillow and watched myself drifting out the window into the dark. I was careful to hold my breath, not knowing which way to turn, until a half-moon showed itself through drifting clouds. The road below the resort ran to the highway leading home, and the mountainside had a terrifying brow. Then I found myself clambering over the rocks leading up, my only map the trail of a brook weaving its way between rocks, its water throwing off silvery gleams as it disappeared below. I followed the stream until it widened, and from there climbed the rocks to a narrow trail following a thin waterfall up toward the mountainous brow.

Then I was on the edge of a stand of trees, struggling to catch my breath, my heart beating wildly. Benny and Karl. Died January 26, 4:37 p.m. Above me the trees, their bare upper limbs branching out into fingers and ganglia, were clearly visible against the sky. I was trying to keep my balance as I inched along like a slug toward the precipice of a massive rock. The resort below seemed small and askew, still ready to collapse. Inside one of the rooms I saw the Nortons asleep, their thick bright-colored tails curled around each other to keep themselves warm. And in the next room was Karl, hugging his pillow like a boy.

Karl was waiting outside my door when I finally got out of bed.

"Did you have a good sleep?" he asked.

"Wonderful," I said as I turned away from his smile.

❧❧❧❧

That evening after supper Karl had them all at his feet. He alone was sitting in a chair, the high-backed one to the right of the fireplace, and the others, even the Nortons, were sitting in a semi-circle on the rug. I was the last to arrive, content to stand in the shadows while he held forth, his words, normally halting and interrupted by the Benny-hum, this time fluent and full, their force, like his eyes, directed at Jim sitting immediately to his left.

"How interesting," Mrs. Norton said, urging him on.

"Is this the story-telling hour?" I quipped as I let myself be seen.

Karl kept right on, not taking his eyes from Jim. "The example of blood relatives is obvious enough, and people are naturally skeptical when it's not a blood relative. But numbers don't lie. They're as hard and clear as what you see on a telephone dial. You just have to keep an eye out for them."

"Do you always start with birthdays?" Mrs. Bronson asked.

"Not always. But you can do wonders with them. Let me give you another example. My wife was born on June 12, 1938, and we had Charlie when she was twenty-six. Now my little Charlie died when he was only twelve – from a meningitis disease – and it left Linda and me feeling... empty, all alone. Do you know what I mean?"

"How does someone ever get over something like that?" Mrs. Norton asked.

Karl looked at Jim as if the question had come from him.

"If we work the numbers out," Karl said, "we'll be able to make the connection. First we see the several twelves. June 12, the fact that our little Charlie was twelve, the fact that Linda was born in 1938 and had Charlie when she was twenty-six."

"Fascinating," Jim said, "absolutely fascinating."

"As if those twelve years fit right into her life."

"Exact fit," Jim chimed. "So it's like if A equals B and B equals C, then A equals C?"

"Yes, it's like that too."

"And everything connects?"

Jim again, still holding Caroline's hand.

"But I don't see where the numbers *come* from," Peter Norton said.

Karl's eyes widened. "Why they come from everywhere. Everything in your life. All you have to do is look around, do some hard and fast thinking back, and translate all the facts of your life. If you've had a life, you can count on the numbers being there."

"And when that fails," I said as I turned my back to the group, "you just make them up."

In bed later that night I still heard Karl's words following me out of the room. "No," he said, "you can't just make them up. They wouldn't be true that way. It would be wrong to just make them up."

❧❧❧❧

Early the next morning, a full hour before anyone was awake, I found myself in my car facing the hundreds of miles between Karl and home. I sprinted the first sixty miles, checking my rear-view mirror to see if a cop was clocking me. But as the miles stretched out in front like a meaningless past, a fatigue set in that lengthened each new mile. Struggling to stay awake, I began counting mile markers lining the highway, feeling a bit more hopeless about ever being done with them as I waited to chalk up another one. More than once I had an urge to stop, pull over and close my eyes, but I wanted nothing more than to be home in my own bed asleep. Highway signs kept leaving me further behind: Drexler 37 miles. Highway 59 the next left turn. Speed Limit 65. And 260 miles yet to go. I stared at the numbers as if I were holding a poker hand. Only two sixes out there. I should fold, throw them out the window by the side of the road, pull over, close my eyes. I glanced at the odometer just as its last two digits were showing sixty. So now I had two sixties and couldn't get around an obvious fact: In another mile I would have even more numbers to make something of. I stepped on the gas and settled in at 73 miles per hour.

When I finally pulled into my drive I could hear the phone ringing inside. It rang and rang as I approached the house, and seemed shrill as I fumbled the key into the lock. I was afraid someone was in the house, even as I entered and stumbled by heart toward the phone. In the dark I took a deep breath before putting the receiver to my ear.

"Benny?"

I waited, hearing nothing but the dial tone, its hum persistent and clear.

# COAT AND TIES

Kate led us into her bedroom and opened the closet door. "All these weeks I've been thinking it might really fit. It seems like such a waste – all his clothes in the closet still. You're perfectly welcome to it."

She handed the coat to Karin, who modeled it against herself. It was both sporty and elegant, its lines trim and smart, its color that of the well-tanned people accustomed to lounging by private swimming pools.

Kate took it from Karin and held it against me. "Gene was tall, but it'll look good on you. Here, let's try it on."

The two women stepped back to size me up.

"Yes," Kate said, nodding her head thoughtfully.

Karin took the cue from Kate.

"It looks really good on you. And it's all leather too."

"It's too good for me," I said as I turned toward the mirror on the inside of the closet door. "I'm not really into clothes. You know, for example, my rule about wearing ties."

"Only weddings and funerals," they chimed.

"But it's a really nice coat. Thank you so much. I guess this is my lucky day."

When we left the room I slipped the coat off and carefully folded it over the back of a chair. Even from there it weighed on me, heavy as the silences that interrupted our attempts to keep our talk light and positive. I was not superstitious about the dead, but I wanted my comment back: It was rash to draw attention to my lucky day in the presence of the woman who had so recently buried the man she loved. Secretly I had wished the coat didn't fit. The final two months were present enough – the way he shriveled and shrank as the cancer spread, eating away at everything but his will to live. And long after I had sunk into hopelessness myself I had watched him deny, then fight, the inevitable to its quiet end. Gene had four inches on me, and all his courage too. In the mirror my face looked good enough, but I felt as if I were wearing skin made baggy by a Charlie Chaplin presence inside. I did not measure up.

He had class. Both he and Kate had been perfect hosts, but I was always on tiptoe alert in their house. The boy taught to take his shoes off at the door had trouble treading on Persian rugs and shiny hardwood floors. And who had ever seen such art outside a museum – ceramic figurines and masks from every continent, paintings and sculptures done in fine detail, and furniture carved from exotic woods that tempted me to run my hands over them. In particular I admired a large cut glass bowl perfectly centered on an ebony table under an exquisite stained-glass chandelier – the way colors from this set played off surfaces in such a way that all sense of surface was lost. For Karin and me the display was too beautiful to touch.

We were surprised when they first accepted the invitation to dine at our house. We nervously put on our best show, the wedding china and silver plate, smallish servings of filet mignon, pasta and asparagus not overcooked, everything served with the most expensive French wine we could find in the store. The home-baked bread is what got to Gene. He kept turning to Karin, asking how she made it turn out, confessing that he was a failure as a baker of breads. I saw her get both shy and coy with each smile she sent his way, and I saw him taken by the black hair and eyes that still melted me. And in candlelight I saw Kate, her lovely features and auburn hair, her serene and intelligent eyes including everyone even as they finally settled on mine.

Of course Karin and I could not keep up with them, their forays to Europe and to the various Isles of the Blessed. They came and went from our lives, every one of their returns generating a new spark of attraction all around. And with every return they made us feel as if they had missed out on the plain living that was our lot – especially the summer evenings on the porch full of smallish talk, spicy food, and home-baked bread.

"Eat more of it," I said one night. "It might help your game."

The game of tennis was a sticking point – for a time. Gene was good at what he did, a natural athlete. He had done his time with a few ordinary sports, abandoning them to master sailing, skiing, and horsemanship. Before we met he already had climbed a mountain or two, and had tried his hand at polo, blackjack and bridge, each skill taken on as a challenge, adventure, and art. So why shouldn't tennis come naturally enough? I let him hack away, silently amusing myself with the notion that this game, invented by his set, was making equals of us while making more of me. One hot afternoon he finally gave up. "I'll never catch you," he said. "Try holding the head of the racket up," I said, "and bend down over the ball." We volleyed back and forth without keeping score, and from that moment we silently changed the rules of the game. "It seems so much more sensible," he said as we were walking home, "to see how long we can keep the ball alive."

That he would actually die was a notion that crossed my mind very late at night as I sped past a small animal, all eyes in the dark, on a highway far from home. On the day the cancer was confirmed he was talking about a trip to the outback of Australia, and a month later Kate sent postcards from Capri and the Amalfi coast. "Capri is lovely beyond words," Kate wrote. "We'll want to come back here some day." Six months later, a week before the end, he had Kate bring to his bed all the books she could find on Tibet.

Before he retreated to his bed he sat in his favorite chair like a king holding court, all of us shy and ashamed as his gaze went past us toward the cut-glass bowl on the table in the dining room. "Everything's happening so fast and so slow," he explained. "It seems as if I'm neither here nor there. One day Capri – and now this *Thing*. There are times when I sit here wondering if this is really my house, and who it is here inside, this *me*. And all I feel is that this *Thing* is happening to somebody else – that I'm the one sitting there where you are watching me, saying look at him, poor fellow, look what's *really* happening to him."

No, the thought of trading places with him horrified me, but I could force out a reasonable response. "If there were some way I could *share* this pain with you... "

He laughed as if he were trying not to inconvenience me. "Share? You want to share? Then where's the hot bread? Why didn't you bring a little loaf over with you? So don't just sit there. There's a nice bottle of burgundy in the liquor cabinet. Why don't the three of you have a little touch."

Kate held his hand like a teenager in love. "We're going back," she was saying just two weeks before he died. "There's a lovely white villa on Capri, and the water is so blue you can see all the way down. The colors – they're something else. Have you ever been to Italy? You'll have to come with us next time." "We'd love to," Karin said. "Mike is such a bump on a log. He'd spend the whole summer on that chair of his, just staring at nothing at all."

In moments like this I too began to believe in miracles. Kate called later that day to tell us she was making flight reservations for Italy. Should she reserve four tickets or two? Karin said sure, count us in, before I had time to wonder who would pay for it all.

On the last day almost nothing was said. Gene, heavily drugged, stared vacantly at the wall as we sat in silences trying to read each other's minds. Kate seemed more confused than despondent, and I kept returning to the asymmetry his absence would create. Karin and I would have her instead of *them*, but who would Kate have? Toward evening Kate and Karin left the room, leaving me alone with Gene. In the other room Karin broke down, her sobs like those of a girl just learning that her lover had run off with somebody else. When Kate returned she put her hanky away, sat upright in dignity, and with pain sculpted on her face smiled at both of us. Gene, suddenly alert, nodded as he concluded his survey of the scene, his eyes telling me how lucky I soon would be to have both of them.

✿✿✿✿

Yes, the coat did fit, but I couldn't be convinced. When I walked out of the house with it I found some images so absurd I closed my eyes to them immediately – the picture, for example, of a warrior walking off the field of battle, holding his fallen enemy's armor high for everyone to admire. I took no such satisfaction from any "victory" over Gene. With the memory of his existence so vivid and fresh, the spirit and flesh seemed confused. Who was *I* in his coat – spirit throbbing inside a fabric of flesh that eventually would wear out, be thrown away? Or was *I* the thing of flesh, the coat a ghostly aura haunting me with a presence more numinous than any memory of Gene could ever be? And if I could no longer locate spirit and flesh, how could I register any proper Christian disgust with the so-called sins of the flesh? I still looked at Karin with plenty of the old lust that holy matrimony had magically converted to love, but suddenly there was new danger in the way I looked at Kate. She had given the coat plenty of thought before giving it to me. Why was I not to believe that she had bestowed on me a mantle of privilege? There was nothing to do but wait for her next move.

Kate went to one of her Isles of the Blessed all alone, an absence that had both Karin and me wondering. "Do you think she has someone else, some stranger who owns a yacht?" When Karin lifted an eyebrow and said, "Why shouldn't she?" I felt betrayed.

In the meantime the coat kept feeling too big. "One thing's sure," I told Karin, "I won't grow into it." I walked more tentatively with it on, careful not to snag or soil it. I couldn't hang it on a hook, because – well, it seemed painful to me – and when I put it on a hanger it seemed too broad-shouldered, present even when the closet door was closed.

"You're being silly," Karin said. "It just *goes* with you."

One afternoon Kate telephoned: Would Karin and I come over that evening, please?

"I suppose I should wear it there," I said.

"Why else would she have given it to you?"

When I opened the closet door I found that the coat had slipped off its hanger and was on the floor in a heap. I brushed and smoothed it out before putting it on.

Kate had them all laid out neatly on the bed in her room – Gene's ties, all twenty-seven of them, greens, blues, yellows, flowers, stripes, paisleys – all of them making a brilliant array on the white chiffon bedspread. "They're yours," Kate said. And as if to persuade me with an irrelevancy, she added, "Most are Christian Dior."

"But I won't live long enough to wear them all," I protested weakly. "You know my rule."

"I know, I know – weddings and funerals. I want you to have them anyway."

I took them away with me and put them in the closet. "I guess I can see it," Karin assured me. "She's got to move on. Having all those reminders of Gene around the house... You don't expect her to just throw them away."

"Did you see all the shirts she still has in that closet?"

"But that would be going too far," Karin said, confusion suddenly crossing her face.

"Maybe she'll give them to you," I said with a sly grin.

Nothing was ever said about the shirts until Kate, out of the blue, resurrected them in the middle of a little dinner for three. "I gave them to the Salvation Army," she said. "Gene kept telling me he had one big thing left to do. He had had his fun. How many people his age had seen as much of the world, or had the chance to do what he did? He wanted to give something back."

"And the shirts are just a little start," I said.

She nodded without making a show of it.

As the weeks passed I saw how determined she was to wear her widowhood casually. She and Karin became fast friends. More than once I heard them break down together in private, Karin's crying now more controlled, like hers. But then the colors returned – the hint of rouge on Kate's cheeks, the bracelets and necklaces, the dresses that inevitably conjured all the ties behind my closet door. They shopped, lunched, took in concerts and films as a pair, and as they became closer I felt left out. "I've never had a sister," Kate said. And one day Karin modeled a new dress for me, a lovely velour full of pinks and blues. "It looks lovely on you," I said. "I fell in love with it the moment she picked it out," Karin replied. "Don't you think it's all *her*?"

My moment with Kate inevitably arrived. Finally alone in the park on a lovely autumn evening, the sun not yet touching the surface of the lake. The trees, massive maples and red oaks, had already turned, and there was a breeze that had the chill of a good white wine. We sat close on a park bench looking at the lake, our hands touching. For a long time we said nothing, even after some kids on bikes jeered at us. Finally, I bent down to look at her face. Her eyes were brilliant against the shadows of her grief.

"A penny for your thoughts."

She looked at me, smearing the mascara under an eye with her sleeve, and gave me a weak smile.

"We were always going to go back."

"To Capri."

"Yes."

"It's here," I said, extending my hand and taking in the trees, the lake, the setting sun.

"We made love on a night like this. It was wild, romantic, wonderful – the last time, really, before the cancer... "

"You could still make love," I said, giving her fingers a little squeeze.

She wiped her eyes again as she looked at me. "You know, I'm not sad right now, here with you. Yes, I could still make love--with you. But there's Karin, and there's still Gene."

"Then I'll wait until I'm more like him."

"Like *him?* How's that?"

"A stranger."

We settled back in the bench and disengaged our hands, and just before the sun completely set we took a long look at the colors shimmering on the lake.

# TRANSLATIONS

Few doubted his genius, but many suspected that he was not a man of God. No one at St. Martin's College for men commanded attention the way Brother Euland did, and no one knew as much about philosophy, politics and art. Whenever students, farmers, housewives, or owners of banks called him day or night, he counseled and consoled, or provided loans and gifts, or held sickbed vigils that lasted for days. Everyone had to agree: He had done thirty-one years worth of solid good works. Still he found time to carve in both stone and wood, and he painted – landscapes, watercolors, still lives. And a special few had heard his poems.

"But I don't know just what it is," one of the brothers said. "He says things that don't seem right. Always interesting things, but I just don't know." No one ever accused him to his face, but many knew that more than once he had been up all night with a widow or troubled girl. "And he lives like a bachelor," one of the younger brothers complained, "in his own neat little pad."

About his piano playing everyone agreed. If under the spell of his music people could not entirely forget, they suddenly were willing to forgive.

When word got out that he had left St. Martin's for an abbey in Mauston to die, and that his death would be a slow and ugly one, people paused to wonder at the significance of the event. Because he was too young to have a cancer inexorably eating away his mouth and face, he gave good men cause to reflect on the mysterious ways of God. His fate seemed too cruel for a man who had joined the brotherhood at the age of sixteen, too unjust even for one who might have tripped over a few sins while performing good deeds on the road.

"Unless God wants to make an example of him," Brother Theodore said, "like Job."

"Or maybe some other example," said Brother Bartholomew, the chapel organist.

It was not permissible for Brother Bartholomew to say what he thought. Brother Euland was a man of genius and art, but did genius and art ever save a man's soul? And who really knew what was blazing in the deepest chambers of Brother Euland's mind, what twists and turns he secretly might have enjoyed over the years? Were there some depths from which there was no return? God knew and could see all things, even those extraordinary depths. Would it be any wonder, then, if God had good reason to silence him in some extraordinary way?

Father Michael, rector at the abbey in Mauston, knew that Brother Euland's death would not be an ordinary event. As the cancer did its silent work, the phone began to ring. Then letters and cards began to arrive, also visitors by car and train, everyone wanting a last audience with him. The visitors left the abbey disappointed and grim, for Brother Euland, his mouth an open cankerous wound, only shifted his eyes when they came near. And his eyes, it seemed, were governed by a precise intelligence that refused him permission to communicate.

Harlan Broder's visit was also a pilgrimage. Like the others Broder wanted more than to bid the man farewell. He too was hoping for a definitive report, the last testament of a man of genius concentrating his mind on the abyss. As an insurance salesman Broder had read too many books to be perfectly at ease about the business of life. He was especially aware of how unreliable the dividends were for those who valued property and life, and, as he settled into a solid but quiet middle-aged success, he was more and more bothered by the question of how to connect the two properly. He had always tried to be a decent man, but was his decency, standard enough in most respects, the only comment his life would make? He had heard rumors that Brother Euland, as if convinced that any words he uttered would emerge befouled by his cancerous flesh, refused to make any comment at all. Still Broder could not help wanting to see for himself, even if the best he could hope for was a sign, a suggestion, a clue, not to the mystery of death but to the moral one could append to the end of an extraordinary life.

In his home Broder had established a separate room to house what he believed was the symbol of his quest. There, centered on a thick Tabriz so that the late afternoon sun slanted in on it, was Brother Euland's grand piano. "I bought it from him for a song," Broder told anyone who asked.

In fact he had paid big money for it, more cash than he had on hand, more than he would have paid for a new one at some music store. On a whim he had answered a simple newspaper ad and driven to an address for a look. The man who answered the door was handsome and muscular, his voice deep-toned and sure of itself, his apartment small and full, graced by exquisite things, all of them the work of individual hands. It was Euland's hands that Broder noticed most as they danced over the piano keys, thick rough hands gliding with precision and confidence, an ease not visible on his face.

"It's beautiful," Broder said of the flourish, only vaguely aware of the darkly luminous burled grain of the piano itself.

"Eight thousand cash."

"May I ask whose piano this is?"

"My name is David, David Euland."

"Oh," Broder said, looking again about the room, amazed to find himself inside the home of a legendary man. "I was hoping to pay much less than that."

"I won't take a penny less."

"It's for my daughter, you see. She's only ten. I want music to be very special in her life. I therefore want a special instrument."

"Right now this piano has perfect pitch." His right hand sprinted up the keyboard and back. "Eight thousand cash."

"I'll have to think about it," Broder said. "Then I'll get back to you."

"So be it," said Euland with a gesture that swept him away. Broder left him standing at the door, his hands in his pockets, a cigarette dangling from his mouth.

As he got back into his car he knew he had to have the thing. But eight thousand dollars? Numbers turned somersaults in his mind as he drove away.

"Why spend that much?" his wife complained.

"I can take a couple thousand out of the bank, and then we can cash in a few bonds."

"The bonds? The bonds aren't anywhere near maturity yet."

"Can't you see? We'll have a solid investment here."

"You can't eat a piano or retire on it."

No, he thought, but it's made of ivory and wood, not plastic or steel.

And he knew how to work on his wife. "It's Julie's future we're looking at – her development and education. Besides, it would look lovely on the oriental rug."

She added a few touches of her own until the finished picture said yes.

When the movers arrived they stood at the foot of the porch steps gathering their strength to go on. The piano, securely strapped to a dolly, looked like an upright coffin the movers would abandon in Broder's house as a practical joke. As they struggled up the stairs with it, Euland arrived in a rusty Ford.

"Come on in," Broder called. "I want you to meet my daughter Julie."

His request was calculated to give the transaction a ceremonial finality. The pianist was parting with his instrument, vehicle of his song. If Euland could be assured that the piano would be in good hands – the hands of a lovely girl who would be taught to honor it – his parting with it would be a farewell rather than dead end. And maybe Julie would sense – intuit – that she was inheriting something grand.

Broder reversed himself as Brother Euland approached. "Or rather, I want Julie to meet you."

Julie finally emerged, but Broder had to coax her down the stairs.

"Julie, this is the famous man I was telling you about, the man whose piano will be all yours. Julie, would you like to shake Brother Euland's hand?"

While the girl dallied at the foot of the stairs, Euland lit up a cigarette. Broder noticed too that Euland's pants sagged and that his shirt was old and stained.

"This must be quite a day for you," Broder said to him.

"Yes," he said, "I've still got two more stops to make."

"I mean giving the piano up."

Euland looked indifferently at a photograph of Julie on the mantel and shrugged.

"Are you moving?"

"I'm going to the abbey in Mauston."

"Will you have a chance to . . . make music there?"

"I suppose I'll pass a few hours translating."

"That will be easy enough for you, don't you think?"

Euland smirked. "Maybe not. You know what Molière said about translation. A mistress – sometimes beautiful, sometimes faithful, but never both."

Julie, her hands behind her back, had cautiously approached, waiting for Euland to turn her way.

"Is it okay right here?" one of the movers called from the other room.

Euland turned away from Julie and walked to the piano.

"It looks real nice," Broder said, dismissing the movers.

Euland sat down at the keyboard and danced his hands back and forth, his fingers sounding a strange melody Broder had never heard before. When he abruptly stopped, Julie, sitting on the sofa in the other room, leaned forward as if something had suddenly gone wrong.

"That was beautiful," Broder said.

Euland stood up. "It's out of tune. You'll have to get it tuned again."

They found themselves on the porch.

"I'll get you a check."

Confusion fell over Euland's face. "I'm sorry, but I thought I made myself clear. Eight thousand *cash*."

"Isn't it the same thing? The check will be good. I'll go to the bank with you if you don't believe me."

Euland looked him up and down. "I was counting on cash."

Julie stood in the doorway, her hands behind her back. As Broder handed him the check, she disappeared into the house.

ॐॐॐॐ

"But I still can't understand," Broder said when he and Father Michael were alone in the abbey garden, "why he took no interest in the girl. Julie is a beautiful child, good-natured, well-behaved. I know she wanted to shake his hand, have him say just a few words to her. He acted as though she didn't exist."

Father Michael's expression hardened. "Maybe that piano means more to you than it did to him."

"I have a hard time believing it – that a beautiful instrument could mean nothing more to him than eight thousand in cash. Cash. No check."

"Did he perhaps suspect that money does not buy happiness?"

"Pardon my asking, but does he *need* the money for anything?"

Father Michael's irritation grew. "Though you apparently do not share our faith, Mr. Broder, you can be assured of two things: That once upon a time Brother Euland took vows of poverty and chastity, and that when we agreed to let him come here to spend his final hours we also agreed to look to his basic needs."

"So he knew when he was selling the piano that he was about to die?"

"He knew."

"So he wanted the money to pay you back?"

Father Michael smiled. "He has not seen fit to inform us of his will in these matters." An idea took shape in Father Michael's mind. "Because, Mr. Broder, you have come a long distance to make this pilgrimage, and because you're convinced that this piano traded in for cash was so special to him, maybe he will tell *you* what purpose the cash is supposed to serve."

Broder noticed that Father Michael's hair was thinner than it seemed, that he was a gaunt and aging man himself. There was a weariness weighing him down, as if he too was preparing to give up the ghost.

"You'll let me see him then?"

"Tomorrow morning. You and I will pay him a visit to see what he says."

ॐॐॐॐ

As the sun was rising the next day Broder bathed himself and put on the Sunday best he had carefully laid out the night before. He waited in silence for Brother Michael's knock on the door, and they walked in silence together down the long arched corridor to Euland's room.

Broder's spirit drained out of him into a bottomless hole when Euland, propped on two pillows in his bed, turned his head toward the open door. Within six months cancer had eaten its way around his mouth and nose and was working its way toward his eyes. A faint stench of decay circulated in the room, swirling in and out of Broder's consciousness.

"You remember Mr. Broder, don't you?" Father Michael said as he pulled up two chairs next to the bed. "He's the man who bought your piano a few months ago. He came here to share some time with you."

Euland found Broder next to the bed, his eyes circling a moment as if sizing him up, then retreating into a passive stare at the wall.

"I thought you might want to know... that Julie – Julie's my daughter, you remember her, don't you? – takes lessons. Practices every day. Your piano – do you remember it?"

Euland's eyes, unglazed by confusion or weariness, shifted, fixing themselves on Broder for a long moment before resuming their stare.

Father Michael feigned levity. "Mr. Broder says you made him a very good deal. He says the piano is worth every penny he paid for it."

Euland's eyes showed that he understood.

"The piano is very special to him. He thinks of it as a symbol of your life, a thing he wants to preserve and pass on, you know, to the next generation."

The dying man remained unmoved.

"As all good things must be passed on," Father Michael continued, "from brother to brother and society to society if, as you know, the work is to go on."

Father Michael waited a moment for his words to circulate in the room, then stood.

"I'll leave you two alone for a while."

The door's closing suddenly locked Broder in. Now and then Euland blinked before resuming his indifferent stare, but never did he give any sign inviting Broder to break the silence they were in. On a table out of view a small clock did its quiet work, its second hand appearing to falter as it worked its way up the dial.

Euland broke the silence by propping himself on an elbow and turning his face toward the wall. He had concluded the interview.

"Yes, I'd better go now," Broder said. He put his hand on Euland's shoulder and gave him a gentle squeeze, but the dying man did not respond. At the door Broder turned toward the bed and had his final say:

"That piano is you – I know it is. Julie is learning how to make it breathe and sing. Someday it will come wholly alive again."

ॐॐॐॐ

Father Michael was waiting outside the door. "Well, what did he have to say for himself?"

Broder, unable to respond, wiped tears from his eyes.

"Did he say anything at all?"

"Is he able to speak?" Broder asked.

"The doctor says he can think of no reason why not."

"Then he refuses to speak – even of the pain, which must be unendurable."

"He refuses all drugs."

"And yet he seems alert, rational... and sometimes his eyes seem to be... scheming."

"You put it well, Mr. Broder. He is keeping very much to himself."

Broder was beginning to see his way more clearly through the shadows of the abbey corridors. What Euland was keeping from them had to be hidden within these walls. He understood Father Michael's desire to know where the money was. There were bills to be paid, debts the individual brothers had to the spiritual brotherhood. Euland had come to the abbey to die, so Father Michael had a claim on the eight thousand cash.

The money matter was vital to Broder, but in a less immediate way. In a sense the money was Broder's too, a matter he had possessed, hoarded as if in a secret part of himself, then passed on in exchange for another thing he could own but never consume. He had paid too much, had not gotten his money's worth, though he would have paid more if required. He was so personally involved in the transaction he could not disengage himself from its legacy. If Father Michael and his brotherhood had no more or less than a spiritual claim on the cash, Broder, as one of the originators of the deal, had an interest in seeing how the buck, as it were, was being passed. In passing his money on to Euland, he was possibly passing it on to Father Michael's brotherhood. Broder did not know if he approved of this end of his own deal, especially since Euland's silence was effectively blocking, perhaps refusing to sanction, any such deal.

Broder and Father Michael sat in the abbey garden again, with Broder aware this time of Euland's window looking down on them. Though strangers, the dying man created a special bond. If they held their silence out of sadness, they also did because they imagined that Euland, as if looking down on them, was reading their lips.

Broder finally broke the silence. "For me it's not so much the money. It's the piano. His renunciation of it was – how shall I say it? – sharp without being clean. It was rough, flat, unceremonial. It struck a wrong note."

"Perhaps you fail to see the real truth of it," Father Michael said. "You take such a negative view of a renunciation that may well be Brother Euland's way, in the end, of saving his soul."

"What, then, does the renunciation mean?"

"Perhaps, Mr. Broder, he finally renounced the world."

"The piano is flesh and the devil too?"

"A man is known by his works. Brother Euland, you no doubt have heard, was a very busy man."

"Capable of sin – like the rest of us."

"He was an extraordinary man. Therefore he perhaps was capable of extraordinary sin."

"Is there any proof?"

Father Michael smiled. "We don't discuss these things. But who can deny the rumors – legends – about ordinary ones?"

"Any rumors about some extraordinary sin?"

"Extraordinary sin, Mr. Broder, usually disguises itself. Or it hides – breeds in the dark."

"What kind of sin would an extraordinary man commit?"

"Haven't you ever heard of blasphemy? The soul's secret cursing of the Lord. The perpetual living of a damned lie."

So all his life Euland had been feigning his call, was no true member of the brotherhood, had been a wolf wearing shepherd's cloth. But at last, just as his flesh was suffering its final translation, he had come home, renounced his old ways, the piano itself, to save his soul in the old nick of time.

"Is there no place in God's wide scheme for the man of beauty and art?"

Father Michael was sure of himself. "Beauty is simple and pure. It is inside of us."

"But his music was simple and pure."

"And his music was also complex."

"Because he was complex."

"Perhaps because he heeded too many voices at once."

"I see nothing wrong with that."

"Perhaps, Mr. Broder, he heeded too often, for example, the voices of lonely women and young girls who may be pretty but not beautiful."

"So if he made love to the ladies it was really all hate in disguise?"

"And lust," Father Michael said.

"But has he ever spoken about these things? Has he ever explained or confessed?"

"Mr. Broder, we do not discuss what a man may or may not confess, let alone whether he has confessed at all. Perhaps a man is best known by his works. Your piano, for example. It is not the only thing Brother Euland has renounced. He also has renounced all relief from pain, and most contact with the outside world."

"All efforts at communication."

"Yes, all noise. Perhaps he is making his peace, voiding himself of sin and the world."

Broder made the next move. "I have a final request. Will you promise me that if Brother Euland speaks before he dies, you will tell me what he said?"

"If the Lord be served, why not?" Father Michael replied. "The truth shall make everyone free."

๛๛๛๛

Twenty-seven days later Euland died, and the merchants of Mauston were overwhelmed by pleasant surprise. Hundreds of strangers suddenly descended on the little valley town, all to pay tribute to the man who was like a saint. In the abbey the brothers chose the gallery to exhibit his work, and there was more to show than anyone supposed. His paintings covered the walls, and there were long tables crowded with the work of his hands – charcoal sketches, wood carvings, illuminated manuscripts in the fine Medieval style done before he had turned twenty years old, and notebooks full of poetry, philosophical analysis and literary discourse. At a separate table stood three stacks of original musical scores. As people filed by the tables their grief was amazed. Euland, despite his rough hands, shabby stained shirt, and half-smoked cigarette, was more extraordinary than they dreamed.

For Broder the abbey itself was an extraordinary thing. As he descended toward the town from the gentle hills surrounding it, the abbey was dwarfed by the grain elevators lining the railroad tracks heading east and west. But when he stood again in the garden looking up at the window behind which Euland had breathed his last, he saw it as a palace in a nameless grand style with far too many rooms to be of any contemporary use. Overhead the brisk autumn sky was brilliantly blue. He caught himself worrying about how the brothers could afford to heat the place once the long winter set in, but the awe that lifted him when he looked up at the perfect stonework of the windows and walls spirited his worry away.

He arrived at the chapel too late to get a seat inside, so he stood with the small crowd at the chapel door. Father Michael delivered the eulogy, but his words, vague like a low organ chord, made no clear sense to anyone outside. Broder caught a glimpse of the casket as the brothers carried it out, and he followed the procession to the burial

90

ground. Before the morning was half-way gone, Euland had been delivered to the earth.

"Is your little girl practicing at her piano every day?" Father Michael asked when Broder caught him at the cemetery gate.

"No, in fact it's a battle to get her to sit a half-hour straight."

"Does she hate it?"

"She only says she does."

"It must be a disappointment to you. You had high hopes for that piano of yours."

"I guess I have no right to expect miracles."

Father Michael paused before a swirl of blazing marigolds. "You've seen the exhibit in the abbey gallery?"

"Yes, I spent some hours there. He did wonderful work – fine, original work. The literary manuscripts are another thing. I was afraid to . . . touch them. I just didn't know how far I should pry. Do you think someone will publish them?"

"Someday perhaps, after they're catalogued and edited. We'll just have to see."

"And you, Father, what did you think?"

Father Michael did not hesitate. "He was a wonderful man."

"You said a lot of good things about him today."

"You sensed them yourself," Father Michael said as he led the way, stopping in front of a plum tree just beginning to turn.

"Who was the Frenchman – the one he was translating?"

Father Michael dismissed the question with a wave of his hand. "Some no-name decadent from the late nineteenth century. A minor poet – I can't remember who. I kept telling him that he'd do the world a favor if he spent his time translating Hopkins into French, but he wasn't one to listen to advice."

"Was the Frenchman a decadent like himself?"

"No doubt. But the important thing is that two weeks ago he gave up the translating too."

Father Michael turned abruptly and faced Broder, as if sizing him up before he spoke again. "We've circled long enough, haven't we? You want to know if he had anything to say."

"You promised."

Father Michael led the way again, silently walking a path that led to the fence enclosing the burial grounds. He stopped at the fence.

"Two nights ago I asked him if he believed in Christ."

"And?"

"He looked at me with those eyes, as if he was searching me inside and out. I had to turn away, because I couldn't stand looking at his face. But for the first time in weeks he uttered some sounds."

"What did he say?"

"He said, 'Once upon a time Jesus must have been a fairly handsome man.'"

Father Michael's words seemed to come out of the blue, a soft *non sequitur* to an argument he had taken a lifetime to work through.

"Is that it? Nothing more?"

"I presided over the last rites," Father Michael replied. "He was awake, aware all the time. You have a right to know that I asked him point-blank then if he believed in the Holy Faith. But he was disinclined to communicate."

"Nothing? No confession?"

"You seem surprised. What do you imagine he would have said?"

"That the Faith is a lovely old fabrication," Broder said.

"You mean lie."

"Your word, not mine."

"Just as his final words and his more final silence, Mr. Broder, are proofs that I, not you, have a right to own. For they prove beyond a reasonable doubt that Brother Euland made his renunciation in good faith."

The interview was done. Father Michael led the way back to the abbey gate and opened it for Broder to leave.

"Good luck on the road – and with the piano too."

"And good luck finding the cash."

"I knew you would not be able to resist probing for it yourself," Father Michael smiled. "Therefore I'm pleased to report our successful results, if only to drive home the final nail of proof in our little debate. I'm pleased to report that we found it last night in a most appropriate place. He left it, Mr. Broder, in his bedpan, all eight thousand in cash."

"I was hoping for something tidier than that. That maybe the cash would round out some new symmetry."

"You needn't worry yourself over the aesthetics of the thing. We salvaged and have it saved. It's still good legal tender."

"I trust you'll put it to good use."

"First, I will explain its significance. Brother Euland, of course, desired to renounce it entirely, the same way, as you know, he had renounced everything else he possessed in this world. Cash is the ultimate symbol of this world. With his mind firmly made up about its ultimate uselessness, you can understand why he wanted to charge as much as he could for the piano you bought from him, and get rid of it all at once." And appropriately he left no note, no word, just the cash. To the brotherhood. We are clearing the matter with the proper authorities and will pay some of our bills with it. Then one day we too will finally be rid of it."

They parted as reasonable men do, tacitly agreeing to bury their differences. As he drove out of town Broder noticed that the trees on the hillsides were ablaze with autumn's yellows and reds, their brilliance leaving the brown abbey in the valley unmoved. The air rushing by Broder's face felt cool and clean. He began scheming of ways to make Julie derive pleasure from her lessons. His high hopes were set, the girl his challenge and responsibility. And the piano would perform its part, especially if he provided some reward – applause, pretty gifts, a small allowance of cash. Ideas came so fast that they carried him swiftly home.

In the abbey Father Michael sat alone on the edge of his bed, wondering how in a letter he could find better words to explain what he already had made obvious. No, he concluded, it would not be necessary to write a thing. Instead he would have to remember to remember Broder in his prayers.

# ONCE AND FOR ALL

Simon Sheftel tried another little lie to get another monkey off his back. "The check's in the mail," he shouted at Hermann Przychiewski, the Chicago undertaker, as Simon hung up on him again.

Simon knew that Lorilee, his second wife, was always listening in, so he made sure she heard him talking to himself. "Here he's screaming at me for his money again. For what? Do I see my mother anywhere? The Polack says hold your horses, she's just lost in the mail. Can you believe these days? He loses my mother in the mail, and wants my money before I see any trace of her."

"Who was it on the phone, Honey?" Lorilee asked from the other room.

"That Polack who ran the ovens at Auschwitz."

"Was that your sister who called this afternoon? Does she know where your mother is?"

It was not Anna. It was Sal, damn her, calling the house again. And as he talked to her he called her Anna so many times he started seeing his sister on the other end. Did he want her to be his bad girl again? Then why didn't he ever come over to her place? Yes, he couldn't believe. His mother dead for more than three weeks, and that Polack undertaker Przychiewski telling Anna, swearing on the Bible, that he put the ashes in the mail almost two weeks ago. "Why should I believe you, Anna?" Simon said when Sal promised she would never call him at home again, "when all I ever get is lies from your mouth?"

At work his boss Jason would sit him down and close the door, tell him about his troubles at home, and Caroline the secretary sometimes cried because Simon was the only one who really cared. And Esther, his first wife, cried a lot just before the divorce. "I tried, Hon," she said, "but I guess I wasn't good enough." Sal cried too, and both Michelle and Christie said it couldn't happen to a nicer guy. His sister Anna never cried, but she carried on. "Are you sick?" she said. "You should go to a doctor for the head. Leaving your wife after twenty-seven years. She was too good for your own good to you. This is going to kill your mother when she finds out."

Right away he married Lorilee, and he never heard from Michelle and Christie again, especially when they found out about Sal. When his mother died of a sudden stroke, he was sure of only one thing:

Hermann Przychiewski came to Chicago too soon after the war and right away made a hell of a success with his funeral home. Suffered in the war, Anna claimed, had to leave his mother behind, and worked his way across like everybody else. Knew the business inside-out. Knew it too well. Because Przychiewski couldn't disguise the Old World accent that lurked in a dim basement past, now and then rearing its ugly head as if looking for the chance to go shouting up and down the streets the way everybody did when the Jews were being rounded up. So why was it so ridiculous that Przychiewski could leave an old Jewish woman in the oven too long, maybe until there was nothing left? That maybe he took a little broom and swept some dust into an envelope so small it could get lost in the mail? Przychiewski had to send something in the mail because he didn't have his money yet. That's the way they were, the monsters who worked the ovens over there.

Anna lived in Chicago, right down the street from Przychiewski's funeral home. Simon made a point of going to Anna's house enough, twice a year, to see what his mother wanted this time. And Anna always stuck her nose in deep where it didn't belong. Why did he divorce Esther, who was such a saint? And who was this Lorilee, a Roman Catholic who couldn't cook a decent meal? Was he fooling around on her too? "Shut up, Anna," Simon mumbled in his sleep. "You think Mother's deaf and dumb in the other room?"

He kept taking jobs in cities farther and farther away, and was thinking of Denver when his mother died. "Why Denver?" Lorilee asked. "Because they got good air there," he replied. "You don't like mountains and air?"

At his mother's funeral he said more than a week's worth of prayers for the dead. "My mother sacrificed her life," he said to the people who came. "She gave her whole life for Anna and me."

She had escaped with her lover from Krakow in the middle of the night, both of them hiding in barns and basements until they reached the frontier. Her lover his father, the one he couldn't picture in his mind, the two of them working their way from the frontier to Amsterdam, from there to New York in a freighter full of tobacco and fish, from the Bronx to Chicago's South Side. The father always gone, working two or three jobs, then one night suddenly slumped in a chair, dead of a heart attack, this man a God to the woman who remained faithful to him all her life, never looking at anyone else during all the years she was still beautiful and young. And Mother never letting go of her little boy's hand when she walked in streets full of dangers and delights, she who saved nickels and dimes one by one, and who when she had enough marched him to the department store for another new suit of clothes. Until he was eleven she held the spoon up to his lips, and he couldn't get out of the kitchen until he cleaned his plate. She marched him to temple every Saturday night, whispering, as she gripped his shoulder hard, "Listen to what the rabbi says, and don't you ever forget."

After the funeral Anna gave him another piece of her mind. "Your mother should be here right now. God only knows what was the last straw – something she just couldn't get out of her mind, something deep inside. 'Where's Simon?' she asks, and what am I supposed to say? That you're moving to Denver with that wife? 'What ever happened to Esther?' your mother asks. Not once she asks me that. She asks me more than once."

"To hell with you! Lorilee's a wonderful wife." To hell with all of you, he thought. Now for sure I'm going to see Sal.

"What are you going to do with her?" Anna asked when they had to work out the funeral details.

"Well, what did Mom want?"

Anna bit her lip. "Cremation."

Cremation? Like her people, in the ovens. Because she and Dad got out just in time, escaped the fate. Mom wants to make a statement with her death, share it with the ones who did not survive.

"Then we should do what she wants."

"Oh you bastard," Anna hissed. "You would do such a thing, wouldn't you? But I'm telling you: You keep doing what you want. You tell the undertaker yourself what you want to do. I'm washing my hands of this whole deal. If you can live with it, then you go ahead and live with it by yourself. The ashes go to your house."

"Whoever said I wouldn't take her into my house?" Simon shot back.

Anna tossed him a look of contempt. "My mother did. Lots of times."

"There you go, there you go again, you who signed with the capo from the camps."

"I told you Przychiewski's from the neighborhood."

"I don't care if he's from the moon! He's not Jewish!"

"You're not going to bury your prejudice at a time like this? Get real."

"You get what you pay for," Simon shot back. "You should know that from day one. Don't expect me to pay half if something goes wrong."

That night he gave everything a lot of thought. When the ashes came he would put them in a special jar or vase. Something really nice from the antique shop, something with inlaid mother-of-pearl or engraved figures doing a dance. And a lid. Where would he find a lid? If he couldn't find a lid he'd go shopping for a little box, one with carvings and a little music inside.

But where could he put the thing? On the mantel in the living room, right over the fireplace. This way when Anna came to visit she would see the thing and keep her trap shut at least about that.

But there was also the extra bedroom upstairs right next to theirs. He could get Lorilee to fix it up – nice curtains and rug, maybe nice new paint, and take that picture of Jesus off the wall. He could put the little box on a shelf right over the bed, keep the door closed so people weren't running in and out. Make a new key for the door. Keep it locked. She could have her own nice place all to herself, right in his house.

Lorilee, of course, would say no. Her picture of Jesus had a right to belong, even though she was always praying to Mary instead. And that was supposed to be a sewing room – and where would guests sleep when they came to the house? Did he want strangers sleeping in the same room with his Mom? What was she supposed to think, sitting there over the bed, if some guests started fooling around?

In the basement there was a trunk full of old things. But where could they keep something as ugly as that old trunk?

Or maybe the safety deposit box in the bank downtown, which had lions on pillars over the big front door. There were some special things in that box – an old ruby necklace Mother brought from Krakow, some stocks and bonds that went way back, the gold wedding band she saved when her father died – all nice things. Maybe the safety deposit box. For sure nothing would happen to her there. Who ever heard of a bank burning down?

But how was he supposed to get any sleep? Here he was again in the middle of the night, and here she was somewhere out there. Air Mail Special Delivery. Registered. Chicago almost two hours by air. So was she in a bag, lost in the corner of some cargo bin? God only knew how many airplanes flew over every night, how many times she had gone back and forth right over his house. Or maybe she was sitting on a table where special mail goes to be checked out with special lights, maybe dogs sniffing all around the bag. How could he be sure of what he saw? There was a little shrine on somebody's lawn – painted bright blue and white. A little bathtub stuck upright in the ground, with a Virgin Mary inside. For sure it wasn't Lorilee in there. And he couldn't remember if it was Sal, because Sal was already too old – thirty-seven years old, probably more. "Not me!" Anna shouted, pointing a finger at him as she ran out of the room, leaving him alone with the family album in his lap, he gazing at the photo of Anna as a thirteen year-old. God she was angel, that Michelle. He could spend an hour just looking at her when she was naked on the bed. But he was always in a hurry to get back, because Mom always needed the sugar or flour or milk she sent him to buy at the store. And you should get a whiff of the bread she baked every Sunday afternoon, how the aroma filled the house, how the bread melted in your mouth if you could keep from chewing it down whole-hog. God only knew who the Virgin Mary really was, how anybody in his right mind could believe in her.

ॐॐॐॐ

"Did you sleep?" Lorilee asked at breakfast. "All you did is toss and turn."

"I'm a Jew," he replied sullenly. "I was wrestling with God."

"Huh? You had such a look on your face. I sat up in bed half the night looking at you."

"Did I say anything?"

"You kept saying, 'Jason, Jason.'"

"Jason? My boss? I must have been dreaming."

"Is everything okay at work?"

"He always expects too much of me. Think Denver – mountains, clean air. A new start. I want to get out of here."

Before he could eat an egg the phone was ringing off the hook. If it's Sal I'll never see her again as long as I live, he thought.

"Is Mother there?" Anna asked.

"It's not even nine o'clock!" he shouted into the phone. "The mail doesn't get here until noon!"

"I don't care," she replied. "I was worried. I had to call. You call me right back as soon as the mail gets to you. I don't even care if you call collect."

Up yours, he said to himself as he, thinking of Sal, sat there with the dead phone in his hand. She's crazy if she thinks I'm going to sit in the window waiting for her.

"I'm out of here!" he shouted at Lorilee as he left the house. "If anybody calls, tell them I'm gone for good."

His boss Jason was waiting at the door when he walked in. "Simon, I need to talk to you right away. Man-to-man, personal stuff. Can you come in my office and close the door?"

"Sure, sure, anything you want," he said as he brushed past Caroline, who was looking up at him with sad love-filled eyes.

❧❧❧❧

All day he couldn't get the dream out of his mind – the way the Virgin Mary came right out of the little bathtub shrine, smiled, held out her arms, and drifted toward him as if she were walking on water or air.

"Simon," Caroline whispered toward the end of the day, "can you and me have a little talk?"

"God," he said, "I'm really busy right now. Maybe we can get together some other time."

"After work some night? I'm really worried about you."

"Sure, some night after work."

Caroline smiled, but when he got home he wasn't surprised to find that Lorilee had not bothered to check the mail. The Wildlife Fund was asking for money again, and so were the Democrats and Republicans. Another phone bill and another offer for another credit card. A coupon book for the hardware store. The latest issue of *Time*. He craned his neck to make sure he got everything out of the box. No Mom.

So what did he expect? To open the front door and find her standing there? She was gone – hair, face, breasts, thighs all gone up in smoke, a grey wisp dissolving as it rose above traffic sounds and disappeared over the Lake Michigan blue. *Shalom.* Blessed be the Name of the Lord. This is the way things were, the way they worked. Blessed be the Name of the Lord. Simon sat in the chair by the window and wept.

"Simon," Lorilee whispered in bed that night as she threw her leg over his, "do you still love me?"

He swallowed hard. "Of course I do. How can you question me when I work so hard all day?"

"I saw you crying this afternoon. We used to laugh all the time. Did I do something wrong?"

"What did you do wrong?"

"Sometimes I don't know," she said, "when you're unhappy, I mean."

"I was crying about my mother. Is it your fault she's dead?"

"No, I guess I don't really think it's my fault."

He turned away from her. It's exactly what Hermann Przychiewski would have said. He was Roman Catholic too. They were all Roman Catholics, the Poles who did what they did to the Jews.

&#8476;&#8476;&#8476;&#8476;

The doorbell rang just as Simon was getting out of bed. The form he peered at through the little window in the door was all too familiar to him.

"Anna!" he said. "What are you doing here?"

She glared at him as she crowded past with her suitcase. "You think it's my fault? That plane circled for three hours up there. Can you imagine what it's like up there all alone when it's so cloudy you can't see what's going on?"

Simon smiled politely. "How nice of you to visit my house."

"I'm not visiting just to visit. I came here to wait for Mom."

"How long is she going to hang around?" Lorilee whispered to him in the kitchen.

"God only knows."

"But you know she doesn't like the way I cook."

"We'll go out – the minute she complains," he said.

"I'm staying," Anna announced, "until Mom arrives. I was going crazy at home. You don't mind, Lorilee, do you?"

Simon looked at his watch. "God, I've got a helluva day at work. Maybe Lorilee can show you to your room."

"Where?" Lorilee asked.

"The sewing room," he replied. "Where else?"

"Do I get to nap in this house?" Anna asked. "You act like I didn't spend three hours in the sky."

"There's a nice bed up there," Simon said, "and a nice reading lamp. And you don't have to worry about electricity here. You can keep all the lights on all night as far as I'm concerned."

They bumped into each other at the bathroom door, just as Anna was coming out. She's getting old, he thought. His kid sister was getting old. There were lines along her brow, and her eyes were hollow and dark. Her cheeks were sagging and so were her breasts, firm pointed breasts that once upon a time he stole glimpses of when she was careless in her bath robe. Her hips sticking out, overgrown, and her ankles too fat. Like Mom's, he thought, just like Mom's when she got old.

"I can't eat a thing," Anna said at breakfast. "I don't see how anybody can eat. When did you say the mailman comes?"

"Eleven-thirty or so."

"Did you call the post office?"

"I called again yesterday," he lied.

"Why didn't you call today?"

"They said they'd call as soon as they knew something for sure."

"You trust *them*?" Anna said. "Look at what *they* do?"

"You want to try one of these caramel rolls?" Lorilee asked. "I made them from scratch."

"Her mother's recipe," Simon said.

"Thanks Honey, but no way," Anna said as the phone rang in the other room.

"It's always ringing," Lorilee said. "And sometimes the person on the other end doesn't say hello. I don't even answer it sometimes."

"Probably that Polack undertaker Przychiewski," Simon said. "You leave him to me."

It was Sal again.

"Are they bringing Mom over?" Anna asked from the other room.

"You go to hell!" Simon shouted into the phone. "I told you I'll call you. I never want you to call me again."

"But sweetie," Sal said as he was hanging up on her, "you owe me a little good time."

"Was it *them*?" Anna asked.

"Yes. That undertaker friend of yours. I told him to go to hell where he belongs. He's not getting a penny from me."

"Maybe you were right about him," Anna said despondently as Lorilee helped herself to another caramel roll. "Still I think before you sit down you should call the post office like you said. Because I'm not going to eat a thing until she's right here where she belongs."

&#10086;&#10086;&#10086;&#10086;

On his way to work Simon saw that the Jews were in the news again. Every day they were in the news, and it was usually some mess. And every day when he walked in the door at work Caroline looked up at him as if he were some sort of god. God, he thought, she'll do anything for me. I wish I could be like anybody else in this place. I wish everybody would leave me alone.

He put his head down on his desk and cried. Where was his mother? He was so sorry, sorry she died. All those years he never visited or called. And now if he could just talk to her once, put his head in her lap.

"Simon, can you come to my office right after lunch?" Jason said, looking very depressed as he stood in his office door. "We've got to talk."

"What's up?" Simon asked.

"It's Susan again. I did a stupid thing. She found out about Bernadette. And now I really need somebody to hold my hand."

In the middle of the night Simon had another terrible dream. He was in Gahenna, right on the outskirts of Jerusalem – down inside a cavern, with fire and brimstone all around. In the shadows Hermann Przychiewski, leaning on his broom, was grinning, satisfied with the way the ovens lining all sides of the cavern were blazing away. Simon looked for a way out, but there was no escape. In the center of the cavern large beasts were moiling in the mud – arms, legs, thighs twisting in the slime like an indiscriminate mass of flesh. "Sal," Simon cried at the twisted mass, "what are you doing down here?" But he was not sure it was Sal, and Przychiewski was coming his way, pointing his broom at him. Simon shrank as Przychiewski approached. "Who's going to clean up this mess?" Przychiewski shouted at him. A strange form began to emerge from the mud. Przychiewski sank to his knees, his eyes widening, and Simon could hear the words Przychiewski silently formed with his lips: "Hail Mary, full of Grace, blessed art thou among women, and blessed is the fruit of thy womb, Jesus."

"Simon," Lorilee whispered, her face looking down at him, "how am I supposed to get any sleep with you tossing and turning all night?"

"I don't know," Simon mumbled, "why you're always praying to the Virgin Mary."

"I told you before," Lorilee said impatiently. "Because Jesus and Mary are really the same. Now, can I get you something to eat? Maybe you'll stop tossing and turning if you have something to eat."

"No."

"You don't eat enough. I'll go down and fix you a little something if you want."

"No, I don't want to eat."

"But I'll fix you something nice."

"I don't really want to eat."

"Come on," she said, "you have to try a little bit. Let me go down and fix you a little something nice."

"But no cereal or toast."

"No, no," she said as she stroked his hair. "I'll fix you something really nice."

ॐ ॐ ॐ ॐ

The next morning Anna left in a huff. "What do you mean, why am I going back to my own house? What if they already sent her back? What if she's waiting there with nobody home? What if there's been some terrible mistake and I'm here instead of where I belong?"

In the kitchen Lorilee was making a racket washing the pots and pans. Simon's headache would not go away. He was too sick to go to work, so he sat in the window and watched.

The dark blue sedan paused in front of his house before pulling away and turning the corner at the end of the block. Minutes later it returned and stopped at the end of his drive. He's blocking my drive, Simon thought. How will I ever get out?

When he saw the uniform Simon's heart leaped.

"Lorilee!" he cried. "They're here!"

He grabbed a cushion, put it over his head, and ran downstairs behind the furnace to hide. Above him he heard the doorbell chiming against the racket of pots and pans. When he heard Lorilee's footsteps heading toward the door, he curled up as small as he could and tried to take slow quiet breaths.

"Simon!" Lorilee called from the top of the stairs, "what are you doing down there? There's some men here for you. They're not going to wait all day. You come on up right now!"

Betrayed, he thought as he climbed the stairs, his legs weak with trembling. At the front door stood both men, only one in uniform, and Lorilee was there too with a smile on her face.

"Mr. Sheftel?" said the man in uniform.

"No," Simon replied, throwing a glance at Lorilee. "You've got the wrong man."

"Does he live here?"

"No."

"We need somebody to sign," said the man in plain clothes. "We've got a package here. We've been looking a long time for you. Would you please sign for it?"

"No."

"We need somebody to sign."

"Why don't you sign it yourself," Simon said to the man in uniform.

"No way. I can't. Not me," he replied. "I would if I could."

Lorilee stepped forward and took a brown envelope from the other man's hands. "I'll sign," she said cheerfully.

Simon's eyes widened. "*You?*"

"Your mother," Lorilee said. "Isn't it nice? Now maybe you can get some sleep."

☙☙☙☙

He was beginning to think he had to do something once and for all. She was in the house again. The brown envelope sat on the desk for two days, Lorilee tip-toeing past to see if he had opened it. He stood it upright on the mantel but it stared at him like the face of a clock telling him he was late. Finally he removed it to the dark corner of a kitchen cupboard, until Lorilee stumbled across it while looking for her eggbeater.

"What do you mean what's it doing in your kitchen?" he asked as she handed it to him. "I wipe dishes in here, don't I?"

He thought of the sewing room, but he backed off when Lorilee began to cry.

"Oh stop!" he screamed. "You know how I can't stand it when you cry."

He marched to the living room and put the envelope on the mantel again. But there were no two ways about it any more: She had to go.

Three times he tried calling Anna, but nobody answered the phone. After the third time the phone rang right back at him. It was Sal again asking if they could just talk. "No," he hissed as he hung up on her, "and not because Lorilee's not home. I'm not here either. We're both gone, so don't you ever call here again."

"Who was it, Hon?" Lorilee asked from the bathroom. "Was it for me? If it's for me, tell them I'm not here."

She was beginning another of her long showers. Then she would dry and fix her hair and fill the house with that perfume of hers.

She found him at the kitchen table sitting with his head in his hands.

"I was just thinking, Hon, that maybe tonight we could relax a little, you and me."

"We'll see."

"I could make you a little popcorn with parmesan cheese sprinkled all over it, and we could just go curl up by the fireplace."

With his mother sitting on the mantel looking down at them? "I'm not hungry," he said.

"I don't know any more why you married me," Lorilee said as tears welled in her eyes.

�����

He sat at the table until he could no longer hear her whimpering in her room. Then he went to the living room and stood in front of the fireplace. There was no portrait or photo of his mother in the room, nothing but silence and the brown envelope with the ashes inside. And here he was – a failure, a fool, an unfaithful man. Esther had been too good to him for twenty-seven years, and Lorilee was another saint.

She even had everything prepared, the fire all ready to go, the kindling, pieces of newspaper underneath. All he had to do was touch the paper with a match. He took the envelope from the mantel and gave it a little shake. A dollar eighty-six in postage stamps. She was feather-light, this woman who kept after him morning and night with the three words that haunted him all his life: "Simon, be good!"

He struck a match. When the kindling flared up he added a log and watched as everything smoldered and caught fire. The neighbors would wonder about the smoke, but they could be counted on to keep their noses where they belonged. This was his fire now, and everything was his fault. So what choice did he have?

"Simon, be good!"

Yes, once and for all. There was a time when they all had to go – mothers, virgins, sisters, wantons, girls, wives. All – and nobody put a stop to it.

Where were the heroes, the men? Where was his father? Where was God?

His hand trembled as he placed the envelope on the fire.

# WAR STORIES

After Dr. Katz died we felt no need to remind Mueller that Katz, though he never went digging for all the details Josef Kubis buried in his silences, was a decent historian. For a time we respected Mueller's desire to probe, his passion for accuracy. He had been born too early or too late to have a war of his own, had slipped far enough down into our historical cracks to have a right to know what was happening to him. But when he began lining his facts up against walls and shooting them down when they failed to talk, we knew he had gone too far – and still had a way to go. So like Kubis we waited for him to learn from our silences, and, given what he did to Katz one night, we may have waited too long.

It must have been Mueller's eyes – full of that bright curiosity we all once upon a time saw in Katz – that prompted Katz to resurrect the name in front of Mueller. "Josef Kubis is dying," he said with a sigh. "That poor old guy. He never did tell a soul."

Mueller leaped at the words. "So let's go before it's too late. Maybe now he'll talk."

Katz, himself feeling frail, went not to listen but to say farewell. As he and Mueller sat in the hospital room beside the dying man, there was nothing to hear except the traffic outside. Kubis, his face turned away from the window's dim December light, did not struggle for breath in his final hour. Curled with his knees to his chest and his hands between his legs, he seemed to be making himself permanently small, his dying the last episode in a long disappearing act. The blanket did not rise and fall with his last breaths, as if all motions of life had come to a stop before their time. Even the clock on the wall seemed to stand still at 4:53 when a nurse came into the room, took a long look at him, and made the Sign of the Cross.

"You have to admit it's something more than odd," Mueller said in the hospital corridor, "why Kubis was one of the living dead for so many years. Did you see him there on that bed – that concentration camp look, those eyes, wide and sunken as if they were trying to hide, back away. Are you sure he was never in one of the camps?"

"No, he was never in the camps," Katz replied.

"Then tell me again, everything you know. I can't help thinking you're holding something back."

Mueller was right. In the forty-five years since Katz had returned from his war as a skinny nineteen year-old, he kept going back to his war, mainly in the comfort of a living room crowded with books that did much to explain why his hands sometimes trembled for no good reason at all. The closest he had come to war was the echo of artillery exchanges rolling off the mountainsides of southern Italy. He wondered if it was his being untouched by any firsthand experience of destruction and death that kept his fascination alive. His reading about the war, begun in a prurient swirl of curiosity, became a narrow obsession that widened into an ocean of information so vast that he, the skinny nineteen year-old, sank out of sight in the war he had skirted by chance. Still there was always one more book to read, one more veteran with a tale to tell, one more secret to unearth from beneath one more tombstone in a village churchyard somewhere on the vast European map.

"We need to talk," Mueller said when he appeared the first time at Katz's door, "because I've been told you know that war like the back of your hand." Katz, resisting an urge to look at his hands, let him in.

Mueller, a reporter not yet thirty years old, had read some of the books. "I'm starting here," he said, "at World War II. Because the survivors are dying out fast, and we owe it to the dead. There are so many stones left unturned. I want to look under all of them, find out who did what to whom."

"Why?" Katz asked.

"Because I'll be damned," Mueller replied, "if I'm gong to spend my journalism logging a lifetime of city council meetings. Stuff happens in wars – important stuff. And people just don't care."

"Why else?"

"Because everyone wants to know who did the dirty work. Because there are people screaming for justice out there."

"You mean the dead?"

"Yes, them too."

"And you?"

"Yes."

Katz gave Mueller one of his long silences concluded with a sad little shake of his head. "Justice? What do you want from me?"

"Everything," Mueller replied. "You can tell me where to go looking for things, the places where no one's been before. Everyone says you're really the one who knows. And they say you know Josef Kubis personally. So maybe you can begin by telling me everything."

ॐॐॐॐ

Josef Kubis would have disappeared had we all not had some place to call home. There's no telling if anyone would have taken note of him if it had been his destiny or luck to rent an apartment in some invisible place. He would have been lost to us then for sure, entirely lost. Katz was not the first to notice him. It was Danko, who owned the corner store. Nobody could walk through Danko's store without being seen and spoken to. But Danko says many days passed before Kubis even nodded his head.

So Kubis was present years ago, long before we realized he was regular in his rounds. For a time – who knows how many months or years? – we were content to leave it at that. Kubis was odd, but he was familiar enough and no bother to us. There were enough people starting fires in enough crowded theaters in the world, and we were smart enough to see that Kubis could be counted on to keep the peace. If he was on the sidewalk with us, we'd mention the weather or baseball scores, and he'd be required to nod or almost smile before walking on. Soon he'd be as safely out of mind as the man on the moon.

But it couldn't go on like this forever, you know. A neighborhood, if it's got any character at all, has its peculiar way of shrinking from a city into a town, then from a town into a village, then from a village to stories full of characters. So it wasn't long before Josef Kubis became one of our characters. Who was he? Josef Kubis. A name we said over and over to ourselves until it almost didn't matter any more. But where was he from? Nobody knew. What was he doing here? Living an extraordinarily ordinary life. How was he supporting himself? A government pension, said Milos the banker, who knew. And every month he put a little away in a savings account. Was he either deaf or dumb? No, but a cat's sure got his tongue.

Why the silence, then? What story was he refusing to tell?

"You know what I think?" Danko said while pointing a finger at his own head. "I don't think he's all there. He's like a shadow on a wall with nobody home inside."

It didn't take long for us to get over even that idea of him. If he was our ghost, we were his. We saw his eyes dart away whenever we glanced at him, and we began wondering how we may have done him wrong, what stories *we* were refusing to tell. But something neighborly had to be done, so a few of us called on Katz, who eventually found out everything we needed to know.

෴෴෴෴

"How did you find out," Mueller asked, "if Kubis wouldn't talk even to you?"

"His silence," Katz replied, "was one proof that he had a certain type of story to tell. All I needed then was a document to make the story his."

"A document?"

"Just about any sort will do. Birth certificates are always nice, though they seldom exist and you always have to wonder about fakes. And passports are hard to find. Tax files, a driver's license, receipts, deeds – that kind of thing leads to other things. I did my share of nosing around."

"What did you find?"

"A medical file," Katz said with an embarrassed grin. "Josef Kubis had surgery in a downtown hospital. No, they didn't cut out his memory or vocal cords. It was a rather ordinary appendectomy."

"So what are we supposed to figure out from that?"

"Where he's from."

"Well, where?"

"Lidici. It wasn't his writing on the form, so somebody else got it out of him."

"Lidici?"

"You have to find an old map of Czechoslovakia, one with all the villages."

"So what really happened there?"

"Does it make you happy for me to go over the same old ground again?" Katz said with considerable irritation in his voice. "If you want to see this old picture still again, I will paint it as clear as a comic book. In the spring of 1942 two young Czechs ambushed Reinhard Heydrich, Hitler's Governor of the Protectorate of Bohemia and Moravia. They threw a bomb in Heydrich's Mercedes, then took refuge in the crypt of a church in Prague. After their associates broke under torture, the two were seized and executed. Hitler was enraged by

110

Heydrich's death. He took out a map and fingered a village. Arbitrarily. Lidici. All the men there were rounded up and shot."

"So Josef Kubis saw it all and survived."

"He was too old to have been one of the children shipped off to Germany," Katz said, as if still piecing the story together in his own mind. "That much we know for sure, and that's probably all we need to know."

"Why not more?"

"Because I've already said too much. Lidici. All the horrible facts are buried in that word if you really feel some need to dig them out – how many dead, their names, how old they were. With that one word you can go nosing around all the graves – but you'll find nothing new. Kubis somehow survived. Same horrible story, ancient as Troy, the same plot, the same results, the same sad theme."

"What theme?"

"Obvious enough--war does bad things to everyone."

"You're holding back," Mueller complained. "There's still something you're not telling me."

Katz tried a smile. "Let's just let it drop."

"Why let it go?"

"Josef Kubis was an assumed name."

"Now you're talking," Mueller said. "He had something to hide."

"And too much to remember."

"I'm more interested in what he had to hide. What did he have to hide?"

"Only the unspeakable," Katz replied as he made his way to the door. "Sometimes memory doesn't serve us right, so please just forget I said anything about this matter to you."

❧❧❧❧

Mueller, never more hungry for what Katz knew, was willing to put up with weeks worth of Katz's mindlessness in order to get at him. Always careful to stay quietly on Katz's good side, he let the matter of Josef Kubis drop for a time, hoping to insinuate himself into Katz's presence during early morning strolls in the park. Katz did not mind his company but had little to say. "I like it here best," Katz said one morning, "when the sky is nothing but blue. There are a few people walking by and dew on the grass. It's so quiet. I remember in Italy... "

He cut himself short, as if he had caught himself in the act of betraying a secret of some sort. Mueller had the good sense not to press him for more. But the next morning he caught Katz on his way home. "Maybe we can get together some other time," Katz said. "I keep getting here earlier and earlier, it seems."

The hour soon arrived when Mueller decided he had earned the right to exhume the dead.

"Josef Kubis," Mueller said in the middle of a silence. "Did you ever talk to him yourself – about *everything*?"

"We spent some time together," Katz replied, "but he wanted to forget the war."

"So you did research... "

"Yes, based on the medical file. 'Lidici.' He must have spelled it out and someone filled in the blank for him."

"When did he arrive in the U.S.?"

"1947 – September."

"And he never went back?"

"No."

"Was Kubis in the SS?" Mueller asked.

"All the children of Lidici, you know, were sent to Germany to be raised as good little Nazis. He was from Lidici. But no, Mr. Kubis could not have been a member of the SS."

"Then he is a survivor from one of the camps?"

"No, only the women of Lidici were sent to the camps. He was never in a concentration camp."

"Then how did he escape, how did he get out? If everyone in Lidici was killed – all the men – how did he manage to survive?"

Katz laughed. "He didn't, you know. He's dead now, isn't he?"

"No, I mean how did he survive what happened there?"

Katz zeroed in on Mueller as he spoke, seeing him as a small man up against a wall, confusion and fear on his face. "I suppose he just saw himself standing there at some point in time, and then suddenly, and luckily, he was just walking away from it all."

❧❧❧❧

Katz seemed to be aging before Mueller's eyes, his figure stooped, his walk more careful and slow. After returning from the war Katz had gone to college, and we were very much impressed by the way he worked his way through medical school. We paid no attention when he started filling his house with books, not thinking it odd that they were all about that war. He was a good doctor, gentle and professional, and that was reason enough for us to let him have his hobbyhorse. If it became an obsession, so be it. He never tried to drag us in on it. Live and let live was what we mainly felt about him.

"But he's slowly losing it," Mueller complained. "Can't you see it? And I don't mean just how he looks – how he's slowing down. I mean the mind, the memory, the way he doesn't go in straight lines any more, doesn't seem willing to talk about things."

"Maybe," we said, "all those books about the war went to his head."

"Think of it," Mueller said. "Everything he knows – all going down the drain. A black bottomless memory hole."

Mueller was feeling more uneasy around Katz, not knowing how to approach, but feeling more and more wronged, betrayed.

"So you're still not satisfied with what I told you about Kubis," Katz said.

"It's obvious you're holding something back."

"You have all the necessary facts."

"But I don't know what they mean."

"*Mean?*" Katz brushed the word away as if it were a noisome fly. "If you had a meaning for your story what would you *do* with it?"

"We need to set things straight."

"Josef Kubis – a broken record, the same thing over and over again. Who needs to hear that kind of thing again and again? What happened in Lidici. It was horrible. So horrible that Kubis was shocked, brutalized, stunned by it, that it was too much for him and he never again could respond, that he slipped into that long dead silence because he was stunned by what he saw."

"And you're saying that's all there is to it – just that?"

"There's always more to it," Katz replied.

"Dr. Katz, I don't get it."

"Because maybe there is nothing to get – certainly nothing from Josef Kubis, who is dead, and nothing more from me. What does it matter? All the facts will never be in. So let's lay it to rest, call a truce, call him somebody's hero and be done with it. And let's just say yes, he was stunned into silence by what he saw. Why not let this be the moral of our story and leave it there?"

"It's obviously not as simple as that. We have a right to know the names of the people involved, their whereabouts, the perpetrators of the crimes."

"Even if the criminals no longer find themselves present in their crimes – if they have other lives, even new faces, in strange faraway lands? If they no longer see or feel what they once upon a time did, even in their dimmest dreams, if all they see or feel now is the grey-haired wife next to them in bed, the grandchildren dressed up for a wedding or school, the sun beating down on them as they walk on aching bones from the house to the church?"

"Are you saying it's just fine to keep passing the buck until no one's to blame?"

"Have you, Mr. Mueller, ever laundered a dollar bill hiding in a deep pocket of your pants? Those dollars never do come out smelling entirely clean, and then you have the dirty water too. All money's dirty, young man. The only question is how old or fresh the bloodstains are."

"What about the men – the ones who were murdered in Lidici? What would their blood say about that?"

Katz smiled. "Their blood is silent now. Like Kubis."

"And what about the children – the ones who were sent to Berlin to be raised as good little Nazis? Where are they? Who are they?"

Katz's smile widened. "Maybe scattered all over the earth. Maybe you're one of them."

"*Me?*" Mueller objected. "Don't be absurd!"

"Are you sure?"

"Of course I'm sure."

"I'm relieved that such absolute assurances are still possible in these uncertain times," Katz said as he rose to usher Mueller to the door, "because that gives me one basis for claiming I'm not Josef Kubis too."

❧❧❧❧

Mueller, again keeping his distance as Katz took his walks in the park, dared to approach one day when Katz was safely waking from sleep on a park bench.

Katz was aware of Mueller's lurking but willing enough to try charming him with our kind of talk – weather, baseball scores, vacation plans. But he shifted gears when he saw Mueller relax and settle in close.

"It's not that I'm getting my hours turned around. I'm always tired, but I seem to need less sleep. At this rate I'll be taking my morning walks before the sun is up. It's as if I'm beginning to get everything turned around. But I suppose that's not a bad way to finish a life. Maybe it's the old age I feel coming on, the mind's way of getting us used to the dark. How it's so dark we stop looking for what we lost. There was a time in Italy. We were going through a little village in the

114

south, and one day the big guns in the mountains had nothing more to say. I remember looking up at the sky, expecting to see the smoke, the faint stench of death in the air, a thunderstorm coming on. But the sky was blue everywhere. I was nineteen. There was a man walking toward me with a mule, and two women in black dresses with jars on their heads. And next to a tree a goat eating grass, and I could see the actual dew on the grass and the goat turning his eyes to watch as I walked past. Can you imagine it? Then suddenly there I was again, lost in some book, trying to remember where I was when I was nineteen, and all I could think about was a sound like a distant thunderstorm, how I could hear the artillery but didn't have to worry because it was so far away. There I was with that book in my hands, a grown man suddenly nineteen again, actually nineteen. And I thought about everything else that was happening then, and I spent all those books putting myself there. And one day I happened on Lidici. One paragraph right there too, with a stain in the middle of the page. I looked it up on a map. So can you imagine how I felt when the war was over and I find myself standing here, in the streets, a nineteen year-old. A big parade for everyone, and here I am on the sidewalk watching the bits of paper floating down. And from then on nothing else matters like watching the bits of paper floating down."

"Even the names of those who committed the atrocities?"

"Especially them. Certainly not their actual names."

࣭࣭࣭࣭࣫࣫࣫࣫

But Mueller had taken to looking for his story in the streets, pacing below Kubis' window, blank thing staring down at him, with the latest newspaper under his arm. We heard him asking around: Did the name Kubis ring a bell? And when we shrugged he began sizing us up, his eyes looking for the hero or villain in anyone old enough to have been there.

He got the answer he wanted in the middle of an October night. A neighbor, hearing glass break in a terrifying dream, was awakened by pounding on a door. Katz – frail, confused and half-asleep – let Mueller in.

"It's about time we get things finalized," Mueller said as he shoved Katz into a chair. "I want some answers out of you."

Katz, too bewildered for words, began looking for a way to escape.

"I suppose now you're going to ask what I'm doing here."

"Well... why?"

"Because maybe we're tired of you singing your little silent night tune. Because maybe the time has come for you to really sing, Dr. Katz – tell us what you really know."

"And what is it you want to know?"

"What happened in Lidici – what role Josef Kubis played there."

"Why, why do you keep coming to that?"

Mueller moved in close, confronting Katz's eyes. "So we can set things right, Dr. Katz. The public record and all that."

"So what is it you want from me?"

Mueller backed away to the window and looked out. "You say Kubis was in Lidici, that all the grown men there were shot. Did you know they were steelworkers, Dr. Katz?"

"Yes."

"Was Josef Kubis a steelworker?"

"Yes."

"And only he among them survived to tell the tale he never told. Why is it he never told?"

"Because his story would have made no sense."

Mueller brought his fist down on a table next to the chair. "What were his real reasons, Dr. Katz?"

Katz stared straight ahead.

"Is it possible that his survival was not accidental – that he was not one of the legendary lucky few who crawled out alive from underneath a heap of bodies left to rot in some forest or field? That he escaped the horror of Lidici by some other means?"

"One way or another he escaped," Katz said. "I don't know how."

Mueller moved in close again, his words a whispered hiss.

"Was he in on it, Dr. Katz – the killing there? He was, wasn't he? He did his share of the dirty work, and the Nazis let him beg for his life? And when he was there on his knees begging to be spared he swore he would never say a word about what he saw and did, and he begged and begged until one of the SS, seeing what a good job Kubis had done on the steelworkers from his own factory, laughed and said let him go, let him go, the puny scum, the miserable son of a bitch."

Mueller grabbed Katz's wrist. "So you're sure, absolutely sure he was a steelworker there?"

Katz squirmed. "Yes, a steelworker. One who survived."

"Yes, and then he had the nerve to come here, Dr. Katz, to live with *us*. And all those years he kept his peace, lived up to his word, puny Nazi scum, the miserable son of a bitch. He was a collaborator, wasn't he? Answer me, Dr. Katz! Was he a collaborator?"

"Yes," Katz whispered, "all the Lidici steel was Nazi steel."

"Yes, and now *you,*" Mueller went on, "what about *you?* You and all your silences, your covering everything up. How did you earn your silences? This business of your being stationed in Italy during the war. Were you a collaborator too?"

"I was a soldier, yes."

"But it wasn't in Italy. You never fought in the Italian war. Isn't that true, Dr. Katz?"

Katz was trembling as Mueller tightened his grip on his wrist.

"*Where?* Tell me, you scum."

"There," Katz said as his eyes finally found what they were looking for. "Yes *there.* Go ahead, have it your way. I was there too, in Lidici – with all of them."

# GODSPEED

Even before he sat down he wanted to tell her to please get off. She was dark-skinned, neither black nor brown, her eyes tranquil and sad. He saw the main fact immediately, the one he dreaded to face: The round swell of her belly taut beneath her flowered cotton dress. And there was no other seat on the train.

"May I?" he asked as she gave way for him to crowd past into the seat across from her. He threw his old leather bag in the overhead, tried to press his suitcoat down with his hands, and then sat down.

Before the train jerked and began rolling he had plenty of time to make up his mind about her: She was between twenty-five and forty years old, she wore no wedding band, and much of what she owned she had packed into her luggage, two shopping bags tied with string. Outside the train window the trees close to the tracks were blurs blowing past. He had seen his share of the world – first by train when trains were the popular thing, then by steamship and then for twenty years by air. In his old age he had turned again to the train, would go no other way, hoping thereby to see a bit of the world he had missed the first times around. And here was this woman facing him.

He felt relief when the blur of trees disappeared to the rear, the view opening into a broad meadow of grasses and weeds. He had the better view, he thought, for he could see what was coming up.

"You going far?" he asked.

"Quite a ways," she replied with a smile. "You ever hear of Money Creek?"

"Not really."

"I reckon not. There ain't much money there, and now there ain't much creek left no more."

"I'm getting off at Three Rivers – just eighty miles down the road. I've got a son there."

"Oh yes," she said, swaying in rhythm with the clacking on the rails.

A fear surged through him as he looked at her skin, beautiful and smooth, and he longed to run his hands up and down her arms. He shrank as she stirred in her seat and folded her hands uselessly on her belly. Composed, she smiled at him before he could escape her eyes.

He had seen too much of the world, remembered even the time before there was a train track running through this part of the state. Towns and cities were hundreds of miles apart then, not minutes or hours. It took days to go from here to there, and one could travel for hours without seeing more than a few souls. Now everything was crowding in, all built up, towns suddenly cities bulging on all sides, everyone going here and there and running out of room.

"Do you live in Money Creek?" he asked.

"Naw, there ain't nothing there. Just my Ma."

She too was going back, also perhaps to pay some final respects, carrying with her that creature still unborn. Gazing out the window beyond the meadow toward another patch of woods drawing near, he saw it more clearly than ever before – his past, a shadowy dynamo that like the train itself had blown him where he was. Another fear suddenly occurred: The train was getting ahead of him, out of control. Could he slow it down, get off in time?

"So were you born in Money Creek?"

"A long time ago," she replied.

Maybe if he asked. Could he please put his hands on her belly, run them over it? He had done it before, when his sons were born – and each time he was afraid they would break like thin-shelled eggs in his rough hands. They held every time, hardening until it was time. And what was it that hardened them? How much knowledge did they have before the moment of birth? How much history in, born, with them? They must have known hardness from the start.

He glanced again at her left hand just to be sure. No diamond there, not even a simple stone or silver band.

"Is your husband hoping it'll be a boy?"

"Him? No, he don't care much."

"He's working so your child will get a college degree?"

"Him? He don't work. I don't know where he's at."

He wanted to move close and whisper to her: No, her husband was gone but he was present too, there, hardening in her. The biologists had figured it all out, the coded history of DNA swelling into new growth from ladders spiraling out of some dim cavelike past. There were others swirling in centuries down there – fathers, lovers, thieves, artists, slaves – all of them by trial and error climbing out of those depths.

"How far along is it?" he asked.

"Huh?" she replied, half-asleep.

"I mean how old?"

"It's gettin' right up there."

"So it'll be born old," he joked.

"But not too old," she laughed. "I been through this a couple a times before. It don't get no easier just because you older, you know."

He nodded and smiled, and she returned his smile before turning toward the window to watch the landscape rush past. In a moment they were among the trees again going by at a railroad rate, she with her future behind her, the rhythmic clacking of the rails beginning to cradle her asleep.

Maybe, he thought, it's like the Bible says: The sins of the fathers visited on the sons unto the third generation. Only three. That would be good, he thought, closing his eyes. We could go on with our lives.

It was her voice that penetrated his sleep as the train rolled then jerked to a stop.

"Suh," she said, "I think it be time for you to be off."

The fear surged through him again. Was it too late? Had he missed out? His heart was pounding as he stumbled through the aisle and off the train. Then he found himself standing next to the track, his old leather bag at his feet, the train pulling away. But all he could see was the pregnant woman and himself facing each other on the train still, he from there smiling as he waved farewell to the old man diminishing as he stood by the track with his old leather bag.

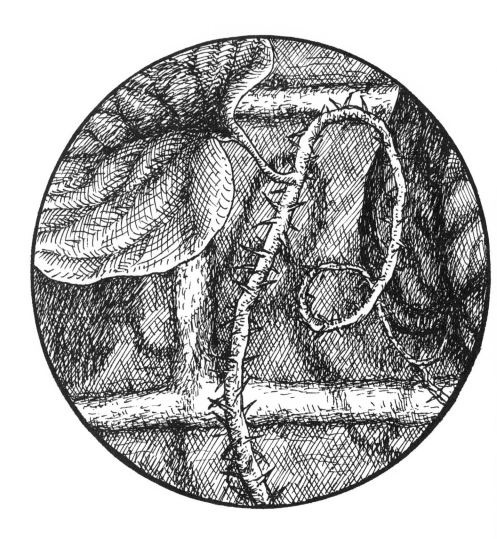

# A MINNESOTA STORY

He had never felt such strength before. He held the rope in his fists and pulled it taut until his hands slid apart over the rough hemp. It would hold. And the beams, walnut timbers he had dropped with his own ax, would show no strain.

He also had built the barn with his own hands. "If you build something," he told everyone who stopped to look, "you've got to do it right. It's got to last." So he didn't settle for pine from the lumber yard. A thumbnail could dig holes in pine. When the neighbors told him he was wasting good firewood cutting walnut for the barn, he laughed and kept sawing away. As the barn went up his fields fell further behind, but one day they saw him nailing down the last boards. Though the extra coats cost him a whole month's work, he painted his barn a white as clean as snow on a cold sunny day. When he was done it was the biggest barn around, and more beautiful, he said, than that other barn in town, St. Luke's.

It was still beautiful. That's why he came to it after turning his back on the radar tower near Jason's Mill and walking across the field to his house, its boards now wrinkled and gray. When was it he decided not to paint the barn or house again? Sometime in the fifties perhaps. And was it because he had no cash or because of some trouble over the price of paint? It was the price of paint, he recalled, as he gazed once more at the front porch of the house he had carried his bride into so many years ago. It *had* to be the price of paint – lousy paint made somewhere in Ohio that kept doubling in price until one day, he couldn't remember what year, he told Clarence in the hardware store he wouldn't buy another drop because he was waging a boycott to drive the company out of business for good.

The years were all a blur. When he was a boy he used to sit on the back of his father's haywagon as the horse pulled him in from the fields, time passing as slowly as the sun went down, his past lengthening out like a shadow on the grass. In those days he had a reputation for being fast – haying, running bases, drinking water from his canteen. His father kept trying to rein him in. "Life is short, and I'm getting too old to be on the go," his father liked to say, "so I'll go slow." After the family bought its first pickup truck the boy liked to sit in back, his feet dangling near the road that rushed out from beneath the wheels and then lengthened out until everything in view, like his father walking away in a distant field, stood still.

It was good that some things never changed. Though everyone had left the old farm, and though the barn and house no longer were white, the place still smelled like the farm he knew as a boy. The neat rows of corn and grain had been taken over by grass that tossed like long hair in the wind, but he heard the same faint hum of life in the air. If he had it all to do over again, he no longer would plow the earth. He would send milk cows to pasture in fields once planted in corn and wheat, and each evening would lead them back to the barn close to the house. We all could have gotten on well enough that way, he thought.

Everyone could have done better, especially his son. "You don't have to see everything my way," he said on the day his son left the farm. "You can learn a lot in college if you keep your head. I want you to learn what you have to learn, go where your heart leads." So he sent his son on his way, and the son seldom returned, not even to visit when his father turned seventy-five.

Because it was hot, the old man told himself, even before the phone call came explaining that it was too hot to be on the road. Almost as hot as July of '33, when he hitch-hiked and walked the hundred miles to Minneapolis to march with the truckers who had come from five states to demand a fair day's wages for a fair day's work, and who, after Governor Olson sided with the strikers against the mob organized by the bosses, danced in the streets.

Nobody danced the way they did, not even during his wedding the year before. When a striking trucker returning to Iowa dropped him off on a gravel road seven miles from his farm, he waved at the truck until it disappeared in the waves shimmering over the road. As he began to walk the seven miles home, he did not feel the abandonment until his farmhouse came into view, its silhouette black against a gray sky, the one small light in the back bedroom window visible from the road. His wife did not come down to greet him when he called from the door, and when he reached the bedroom she only half-rose from her pillow to look at him. "Are you finally back?" she asked as she put her head down again.

He wanted her to ask. He had rehearsed it all as he and the Iowa trucker sat in silence watching the cornfields drift past. He would not tell her he had walked almost thirty of the hundred miles before a farmer stopped to pick him up, or that he had not slept in two nights.

He wanted to tell her how the men, many with their wives, found each other, how they developed one mind and heart, and how at the end of the second day they were cheered by the soldiers who turned to confront not them but the jeering mob. As he stood before her unbuttoning the only shirt he had worn those three days, the only white shirt he owned, he wanted to tell her about the new hope that had surged into his life. But as she reached up to turn off the small light, he saw not only weariness on her face but a resentment heavier than the jeers left behind on the streets.

In town the next afternoon, people turned away or crossed the street. They think I betrayed them, he thought – believe that because the truckers got more, the farmers got less. He was a farmer too, so he knew about getting a fair day's wages for a hard day's work. He talked and pleaded and talked, and everyone agreed he stood up for his beliefs. Besides, he had a way with crops, cows, and machines, was always willing to lend a neighbor a hand or his old Fordson, which he kept shined, tuned and full of gas.

When he ran for the town council they didn't put anyone up, and later when he ran for county commissioner they secretly voted for him. He resigned one day in the middle of his second term. "Because you don't want real change," he said. "And besides, I've got better ways to spend my life." He began taking trips to Minneapolis during the winter months. "To go to meetings," he told them when they asked. "Do you think things just run themselves? Do you think the world will change without planning how? There's such a thing as tactics and strategy, you know."

One day a grain buyer pointed at him. "They have meetings up there," the buyer told farmers with grain to sell. "They're radicals."

Now and then someone called him a communist, and then they backed off. One day he found an effigy of himself hanging from an apple tree behind the cafe, but he just laughed and turned away. When the things he said were quoted in the newspapers of bigger towns, almost everyone was just a little proud of him.

He was a big grey man. Even before he was married his black hair was streaked with silver, and by the time he was forty it all had turned. He had spent one year at the university before his father, ill and tired, called him back home to farm. Someone said that he came back full of complaints about religion, the government and the town itself – claimed there were no books worth reading in the schoolhouse or library. He seemed to grow taller and stronger as he settled into farming, his hair wilder and whiter, and after he was married he didn't

125

show up in town for six months, his wife still driving the old pickup to the IGA and St. Luke's, as she always did, alone. But one day he walked into Byron's Cafe wearing a white shirt and the old black suitcoat his father used to wear, and under his arm was a big black book. Someone said he looked like a preacher, and everyone laughed.

The old black suitcoat and white shirt became his uniform. "If you think I'm a preacher, why don't you listen to my word?" he asked the men in Byron's Cafe. "You'd rather give your souls and money to those monkeys who pray to their white God to complain about you having a little fun. And when the price of corn goes down they tell you to count your blessings instead. Your preachers are your bosses, and they're so good at it they make you feel bad about what's fair and good."

"That's right," some said. "That's *damn* right." But later they told each other they only said it to get rid of him.

There was a lot of talk about his wife, especially about how he kept up the talk while she kept up the farm. Except in her last year she too was tall, hard and grey, and good-looking enough to make men turn away when she walked by. Unlike other mothers in town she had no son to give to the war, but his going off to college took its toll. Her husband was gone more and more, and someone said it was his way of leaving her. She died without warning in the spring of 1959, having failed as fast as the snow melts off the fields. With her the people of the town buried the story of her life. When they meandered home after the funeral, they left her husband standing alone stone-faced at her grave.

He was alone on the farm seven years after that. Because he never had a hired hand, and because the farm showed no signs of decline except the fading white paint on the house and barn, the town stopped accusing him of working his wife to death. One day he announced that he was through, that all he needed any more was a room in town and fifty dollars a month. "When I sell my cows and tractor I'll be rich," he said. "We all make a religion of work. There's another kind of work that needs doing before I leave the scene."

When he took his apartment in town, a makeshift place over the hardware store, he made sure it had a window facing west toward his fields. From the farm he brought a brass bed, Victrola, library table, lamp, and chair. He closed the door and turned on the light that was always on late into the night.

Nobody came knocking, thinking of his place as a closet full of forbidden thoughts. Now and then his son visited him at the farm.

"He's tired of counting someone else's money, and tired of all that traffic noise," the old man said with a curled smile suggesting that he was beginning to taste victory. "He'll come back. You'll see."

He did come back, parking his Buick outside the hardware store, and it didn't take long for people to know something was wrong. Everyone could hear the shouting, father and son in the street having it out. "Over my dead body," the old man yelled as the son opened the door to his car. "I'll give it away before I see it sold. A hundred years from now my ghost is going to live on that land, even if you won't. I've got my will all made out, and I'll carry it here the rest of my life, in my shirt pocket, right over my heart." Whatever else he said was lost in the roar of the engine as the Buick sped away.

"I'll be goddamned," the old man said as he turned away from the Buick, "if they taught him anything at college but how to count money somebody else didn't work for to earn."

≈≈≈≈

He disappeared into his room above the hardware store, coming out only to take a sandwich and soup at Byron's Cafe.

"What do you do up there all day?" they asked.

"If you want to get from here to there," he replied, "you have to think it through. I'm writing a book."

A week later they found him hunched over a bowl of soup, a book next to his fork.

"Poems," he said.

They quietly backed away.

"What's the matter?" he shouted after them. "Are you afraid? There's a war going on, a dirty little yellow war that's eating up billions of dollars and thousands of lives – and here we just sit around and grumble about the price of beans. Do you think we can get from here to there by just standing around?"

He got so loud that Byron came out of the kitchen to tell him he'd better go home. Instead he went to a bar down the street, concluding the night with a shot of whiskey from his own flask.

He ended his boycott of Byron's Cafe on a winter night, showing up late when nearly everyone else was gone. He looked exhausted, skinny and pale, and his hand trembled as he lifted the spoon to his lips. Twice he stumbled on the way out, and he did not object to Byron taking him by the arm to his room above the hardware store.

As Byron came down he was met by a woman getting out of the old man's pickup. She was in her thirties and had been in town before – standing on the periphery of a crowd during a speech the old man was making in the park on the Fourth of July. She was good-looking enough, Byron thought then, though a bit heavy all around and wearing a smile too relaxed for someone new to the town. When they met at the door she wore no smile. She stopped and eyed him suspiciously up and down.

"Is he up there?" she asked.

"In bed," Byron said.

"He needs someone to take care of him," she said as she brushed past.

The next morning she appeared in the cafe and made her announcement out loud: "He's dying," she said when all the faces turned her way. "He didn't want me to say, but I think it's best that you know the whole truth about him."

She glared at them accusingly until someone finally spoke.

"Is there anything we can do, Missus?"

"You keep away from him – that's what you can do. He ain't happy about going and he's too much a man to be afraid. Let the man have some peace."

When she closed the door of the cafe they all felt as if she had slammed his coffin lid in their faces. They watched her come and go from his place, all but ignoring news about the radar tower fallen down by Jason's Mill. In the low hum of the cafe broken only by the wail coming from the pink juke box, they began talking about all the things the old man used to say.

Then on a Wednesday afternoon the door of the cafe opened and a little cheer went up. Though still pale, he looked like a shaggy Moses carved out of stone. "My God, he's got a beard now too," someone said.

"It's not old age you're looking at," he shouted back. "It's what you don't see that counts. This white hair has roots that go way down."

They laughed. "Well, where have you been, old man?"

"You think just because a body isn't running it's standing still, that if things stand still long enough they'll just go away? No wonder we've got a police state coming on. No wonder we don't pull together according to how much we weigh. You think pulling together means being led by the nose. Where have I been? Doing my work, having a little excitement in my life. Up in my room trying to get from here to there. Where else?"

He took to hanging around the cafe waiting for someone to come in. "The war," he started in, "how are we going to put a stop to that dirty little yellow-bellied war in Vietnam?"

His talk about the war went on and on, so there was talk about keeping him from hanging around the cafe. The town was also beginning to have second thoughts about what had happened at Jason's Mill, the farm next to his own, on the very night he turned up pale and sick. When the townspeople heard about how the radar tower had been chopped down with an ax, they pointed the finger at him. No one accused him directly when federal agents arrived to snoop around, but a few told the agents to check him out. "But yes," they all agreed, "he was real sick that night," probably too sick to swing an ax against steel cables more than an inch thick.

Yet they all knew he somehow had given the tower a push. They all remembered his speeches against the tower going up, and sure enough when the big machines rolled up to Jason's Mill to build it there his old pickup was on the gravel road blocking the way. The younger Jason even pointed a shotgun at him and bought three Dobermans to keep him away. "He said I had no right to the property if I was going to let them build that thing on it," the Jason boy told the sheriff. "He said he had as much right to my property as I did. He said property is theft. That's when I got the dogs."

"Sellout," the old man said in the cafe. "The Jason boy is selling out the land right out from under us. Their steel trampling on our corn. No memory. If I asked him whose side the army was on in the strike of '33, he'd think I was talking football, and if I said Wobbly he'd think I was talking about weak legs. But I guess he's only like the most of us. First we let them take our boys like lambs to slaughter in a chickenshit yellow-bellied war, and now they take our land. Someday they'll turn all this pasture into a battle zone. They're thinking big these days."

A new tower was up within a year even though again they found the old man's truck blocking the road, and the agents didn't take him away. So, everyone concluded, he was either a lot smarter or less guilty than they thought.

঩৵঩৵঩৵঩৵

It was the middle of an October day when he climbed into his pickup to return to the farm. The old truck, rusty on all sides, sputtered

129

haltingly as it started up. The mailman saw the pickup on the edge of town, and waved as he did to anyone passing by. Within a minute the town was small in the rear-view mirror, only the grey grain elevator visible on the horizon, the road behind him disappearing into fields of drying corn. Framed in thick glass, a world of wildflowers in the ditch rushed by like a golden blur, while an oak in the middle of a cornfield stood in solid silence drifting out of view. Beyond the oak the hills on the horizon seemed to flow forward like a green glacier returning from a distant sea.

"Maybe I should have left long ago," he told himself. "Maybe I should have sold the land right after she died. I could have lived in a city somewhere, maybe with a few of my kind." His thoughts failed as the pickup slowed to a walk behind a haywagon straddling the shoulder and road. As the wagon turned off, the big grey radar tower became visible on the horizon, as did two hitch-hikers. The pickup came to a stop, and before saying a word two boys in their late teens threw their bundles in back and climbed aboard.

"Where you headed?" the old man said.

"The city." The one who spoke had hair to his shoulders. "Don't suppose you're going that far, are you?" The boy grinned broadly, showing a row of white perfect teeth.

"No sir, I'm just going home – a little ways up the road."

"Hey, old man, you should take us all the way. We ain't gonna get no ride out of a hick town like this." This one, dressed in jeans and a flannel shirt, did not smile.

"Where you two from?"

"Pine River," the longhaired one said.

"No school these days?"

"We're all done with that," the other said.

"Then you work?"

The boy with the long hair widened his smile. "No man, we're *bored,* old man."

"You're going to Minneapolis?"

"Right, man. The Jefferson Airplane is coming tomorrow night."

The old man's face winced in perplexity.

"The Airplane, man," the boy in the flannel went on. "They ain't as good as The Association, but they're all we can get in these hick parts."

"He don't know what you're talking about."

"Hey man, a group. The Airplane's a group."

"A group?"

"A rock group, man. Where you been all your life? You know –
sha-boom, sha-boom. You remember now?"

They both laughed, and the old man forced a grin.

"You never listen to rock, old man? Ever hear the Airplane? It's
good for your soul, man."

He thought of the old Victrola, the dog with its ear to the speaker.
"No, I guess I don't prefer that kind of music. But once I heard the
orchestra play. It was many years ago, and that was good for my soul."

"Where'd you hear it, old man? In the park?" The longhaired boy
laughed.

"I bet he ain't never been to Minneapolis," the one in flannel said.
"I talked to lots of farmers who told me they ain't never been to
Minneapolis. That's no lie."

"Yes, I've been to Minneapolis," he said. "When I was young like
you I hitch-hiked up along this road."

"Did you hear the blues? They had blues in your day, didn't they,
old man?" the longhaired one asked.

"No," he replied, "I went to a strike."

"A *what*?"

"A strike. A protest."

"You mean a demonstration."

"Yes, a demonstration."

"Never had one in my school."

"Why not?"

"I told you – there ain't nothing ever going on."

"And besides," the boy in flannel said, "the teachers are so dumb
they'd call out the National Guard."

"Doesn't that make you see red?"

"It don't do nothing, man."

"You don't like politics?"

"They're all in it for themselves. I say who cares, as long as they
don't bother me. Live and let live – that's what I say." The longhaired
boy relaxed into his seat, well-satisfied.

"But we never turn down no partying," the boy in flannel said.

"And you didn't like school?"

"Booored. Eight hours a day, five days a week."

"Why's that?" The old man lifted his foot from the pedal a bit.

"These hick towns. There ain't nothing happening here. There
ain't no one more interesting than us – and that's because we go to the
city every time we get some loose change – and there ain't nothing
louder than the sound of growing corn."

"You left out my pig," the smiling one said. "My pig Sally's more interesting than you, and when she's in heat she makes more noise than a county full of growing corn."

"You can stick your pig," the other said, "and someday I'll eat her."

"She'd be better than that fat one you're screwing now." The two of them laughed again, but he didn't hear the laugh, just as he didn't hear the pickup strain under the weight of his foot as he pressed the gas pedal to the floor; and as the truck veered onto the shoulder of the road, he didn't see the ditch until the longhaired boy grabbed his arm. In the next moment the three of them were sitting in silence, looking up at the road from the ditch, all of them stunned and trembling.

He felt the fear most when he stood next to the truck, his legs suddenly elastic and weak.

"You all right, old man? You look pale as a ghost."

"I'm just a little wobbly." He smirked at his private joke. "I'd hate like hell to go this way, especially at my age."

"You want me to drive now, old man?"

"No, I prefer not to." He climbed into the truck and started it. After saying some things to each other, the boys also got in.

"You slow down now and stay on the road."

"Yeh man, I ain't got but one life to live."

"You see, old man, my buddy here had an older brother killed in a car accident last year. He got blitzed one night and run himself into a tree. It was a tragedy."

He drove a quarter-mile before anyone spoke again. Then, as if from nowhere, the words came. "It was no tragedy," the old man said. "It may have been sad or too bad, but it was not a tragedy."

The words were spoken quietly, addressed not to the boys or to himself or even to the air rushing past. The boys looked at each other, shrugged. A few minutes later the old man came to a crossroad and the boys climbed out. As the old man drove off he looked into the rearview mirror at the boys walking backward down the empty road, their thumbs begging a new ride.

He parked the truck in the middle of the gravel drive leading to his house. On the grass near the house he found himself breathing the fragrant air deeply in and looking at the Norway pines surrounding the house. To the right he saw his two hundred acres bathed in the soft colors of a setting autumn sun, the yellow grass flowing in the breeze like currents on a wide river. A quarter of a mile on his left the grey radar station, its legs lost behind a hill and its head slowly scanning the sky, stood like a steel giant near the old stones that once had been

132

Jason's Mill. He saw near there the walnut grove where he had dropped the logs for his barn. A fifty year-old shame returned as he recalled the lie he had told his neighbors. "I told them I was cutting the logs to clear the acres," he said to himself, "but we all knew I just wanted to have the best barn in these parts." He looked at the barn. Even with its weathered boards it looked solid and strong, no sag visible anywhere in the roof. "And it's still the best barn in these parts. They said I'd kill myself finishing the thing, but then they said I wasn't healthy enough to finish another job too."

He began walking across the field toward Jason's Mill. Halfway to the tower he stumbled across an old hickory fencepost lost in the grass. He picked it up, beat the air with it once, then locked it in his fist and carried it like a club. When he reached Jason's wire fence he used the post to hack his way through, his heart pounding as the tower inched higher and higher into the sky with his approach. At the top of a rise the whole tower came into view, its legs wide on the ground and its superstructure supported by thick cables emanating in all directions toward concrete cubes planted in the field. The old man paused a moment at the summit of the rise, his form outlined in black against the setting sun. Then he began walking closer to the tower until he came to the fence surrounding it. A sign in black and red glared out at him: DANGER KEEP OUT. U.S. GOVERNMENT PROPERTY.

There was a time, he thought, when they didn't have a fence. You could just walk up to it like a bully who lived next door, and you could talk to it. Now you can't get near enough to reach one of the cables, and if I touch the thing I suppose it'll take my picture and fingerprints. I suppose they're watching me right now – suppose they have been for a long time now. Me – who couldn't handle a wife and didn't know how to keep a son on the farm. And now what? Throw sticks and stones at it? Write a letter to my congressman? Go home and pretend to forget everything I know and believe?

He lifted the post over his head with two hands, and brought it crashing down on the fence. He felt the old strength return, the hickory post feeling as light as the ax that once upon a time cut through the cables holding up the tower. Each time he struck the fence he saw the sparks the ax let off, and he heard the sharp snap the cables made as they burst free into the air. And he remembered his hands stung numb from the crash of steel on steel, the way the superstructure began to totter like a drunken man, lost its balance against a sky full of stars, and fell. And there was no explosion when it hit the ground, everything on the grass suddenly going silent as if the earth were his co-conspirator. It was easy, he thought as he rubbed his hands to get feeling back, and, careless even of the tracks he left behind, threw the ax over his shoulder and walked away.

Maybe too easy then. Even the agents the government sent out were city slickers who didn't bother looking for anything in the grass, they all dressed up in their suits and ties. Now the fence had a few dents in it, but it had not buckled or given in. They would come for him this time. He took one last look at the tower, threw his hickory post at the foot of the fence, and began walking home.

By the time he reached the old farmhouse the crickets were singing in full chorus and the sun was sinking beneath the horizon. He stood a moment looking at a broken window in the old house, a chill passing into him. I'll have to fix that before the snow starts to fly, he thought as he turned and walked toward the barn. A vague fear that he had lost something stopped him at the door of the barn. When his hand found the old will in the pocket of his shirt he froze. "Yes, of course," he said to the ground as a notion gripped him from behind, refusing to let go now that it had finally caught up. "It's the only way. What else will wake them up? There's nothing waiting for us now but old age and accidents. No one will bother to crucify us any more."

He paused before he walked on, his motionlessness as frozen as the notion that had entered his mind. He looked at the old haywagon still outside the barn, the swing made of the old tire still strung to the branch of the oak, his son a little boy going back and forth, back and forth, laughing as he went higher and higher. And there was the house itself, once bordered on all sides by flowers in perfect rows. A bird scrambling near the top of the barn door broke his reverie, found an opening, and flew away.

"No sense going back to Byron's," he said. "No one listening to me there. They'll just make a bigger and bigger fool of me."

He turned and walked into the barn, his gaze immediately turning upward to the beams as if he were a child entering St. Luke's. He found the rope precisely where he had left it years before. Yes sir, he thought as he threw it over a beam near a white stool that he and his father once had used for milking cows, it would hold. He was pleased to find in his coat the pen he always carried to write down thoughts. From his shirt pocket he took the will and bent down on one knee. "It's hopeless," he wrote across the will in a clear bold hand.

As he folded the paper he gazed at the faceless head of the tower near Jason's Mill. Then he placed the white stool under the rope, and, testing the balance of the stool, with steady legs stepped onto it.

# REUNION

The hour of his thirty-year high school reunion closed in on him like the moment he danced his final dance with Victoria at their senior prom. He was bewildered when she pressed her body close to his in a way she never had before. In his father's new '55 Ford that night she swore it was love, but morals were morals and again she said no. "Remember how we swore we'd never be like everyone else," she said, "how we'd live up to our ideals?"

They parted company, he to a village in Nigeria where he helped the people put in new wells, she to a master's degree in teaching the verbally impaired. After four years nothing surprised him in the hot African sun except the news that she had married an executive vice president of the World Bank. He worried about only one thing: Would she somehow be spoiled?

At the reunion he wandered off like one lost among the kinder animals in a zoo, faces everywhere nameless but somehow known, familiar outlines still visible inside sagging and overblown flesh. He, one of the few who had kept his shape as lithe as his beliefs, seemed entirely out of place and was speechless in a room full of talk too, too small.

Their eyes found each other's immediately. Once more he stole glances at her breasts and slender hips, and his heart, his heart, once more beat like a boy's.

"Come on, let's dance," she said, grabbing his hand. Within an hour they were alone in her suite, exhausted and naked on her bed.

"I've got to know," he said, "before I let you go again. Did you do it?"

"*It?* What do you mean?"

"We were going to change the world."

"Oh yes," she said. "Everything's different now."

"I mean – what do you... *do?*"

"Oh darling, it's real estate I do. Manhattan real estate."

He was suddenly aroused again and reached over to fondle her.

She giggled. "You want to do it again?"

And suddenly he couldn't think of any other name for it.

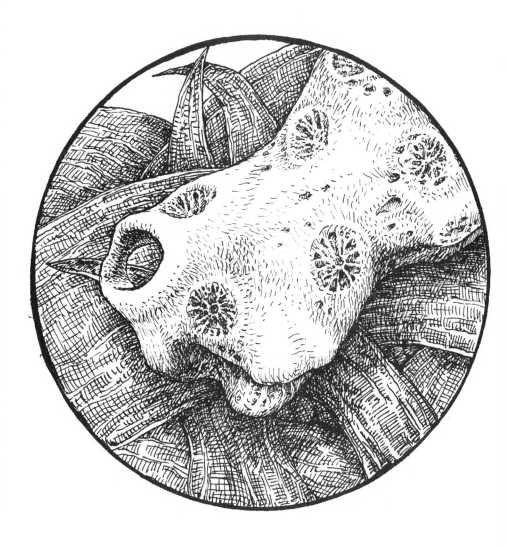

# NINE-TENTHS OF THE LAW

"So, don't you think we've come a long way in the last few months?" she asked from her hospital bed as he took hold of her hand again. Though words still did not come easy for her, she managed a smile he had taken for granted until recently. In a roomful of faces hers had been invisible, her high cheekbones and deep-set eyes lost behind the fact that she was middle-aged, overweight, and not good-looking at all. So for weeks she was there and not there, vaguely there when she was looking at him, absent as soon as he looked the other way.

Now that she was slipping so quickly away she would never fully know how far that long way had been for him.

"Yes," he replied, feeling the inadequacy of his words, "it's been a privilege to become your friend."

After her funeral he had a special ceremony of his own. In his back yard, next to a garden plot he had tilled for years, he dug a small firepit, circled it with loose stones, and built a pyre of dry leaves and twigs. From its place in the china cabinet he took what he had come to call simply "The Book," and he reverently placed it in the firepit. The leaves caught quickly and soon the little pyre was ablaze. He watched until the flames died, revealing the volume still intact at the bottom of the firepit, its edges charred and smoldering. With his hands he threw loose dirt over it until there was no sign of book or stones. Then he went inside and watched as clouds formed and cold rain began to pour down.

Again and again he remembered her as the presence standing to one side waiting for him to finish with everyone else, the one who, when her turn finally arrived, shied away, lost for words. "Can I help you?" he first asked, hearing his words make a customer of her. She blushed and almost dropped the books under her arm, taking two steps back as she spoke. "No... I don't know," she managed to say, "I just wanted to... listen. Everything you say is so interesting."

He resented the comment because it too put pressure on him. There was another woman in the room, Laura Lambeth, auburn-haired, sleek and beautiful, reacting with arch indifference to him.

"I mean... I didn't know you could get so much out of a book."

"Is this your first college class?" he asked.

"I started once, but that was a long time ago."

"It's never too late to learn a new approach to things."

She smiled as she tucked her books back under her arm. "Is there anything I can do – I mean, to get something out of what I read?"

"Just read everything carefully a couple of times, and if you don't get it read it again."

"Should I maybe underline special things in the book?"

"Oh no, never do that," he replied. "Books are very special things, especially if they're old. Would you write on the walls of a church? I hate to see books all messed up."

"I never thought of that," she said with a quiver of embarrassment in her voice. "I guess I've already messed mine up."

"By the way, I don't have your name down yet."

"Oh," she said, offering him her hand to shake, "I'm Dolores."

"Dolores – is that the long and short of it?"

His question drew a blank from her.

"I'm Dolores Johnson. You can call me just Dolores if you want."

જ•જ•જ•જ

The night he came into actual possession of The Book – that is, held it in the privacy of his own home – it became obvious that possession was nine-tenths of the law. What right did Dolores Johnson have to The Book after she placed it in his hands and insisted that he take it home with him? Was it not therefore his until she demanded its return? He slept comfortably that night, The Book on the table next to his bed, and when he awoke the issue presented itself in new, this time practical terms. The Book could never mean to her what it meant to him. From its pages, written in a Latin even he barely understood, she would draw nothing but blanks. In time he would get its gist, but how would anyone benefit if it remained in her hands?

From the beginning he had tried distancing himself. As he saw her leaning in to catch his eye he, in his well-practiced professional way, skipped over her. She waited her turn, which seldom came around, and she waited for him after class, unable to speak unless spoken to. He dreaded their encounters at the door, her presence there at the end of each hour that of a gatekeeper blocking his escape into the world. He had his ways of getting out, appointments at ten and other things to do, and once, just once, he told her he didn't understand what she was trying to say, that she should come back when she had thought it all out.

The next day she was waiting for him again.

"Well," he asked, "what can I do for you now?"

"Would you like to come over some night?"

Her words got lost in the gleam of Laura Lambeth's hair as she brushed past. "Well, yes – some night. That's awfully nice of you."

"Friday night?"

"I'm sorry," he lied, "but I've made other plans."

"Then you just name a date," she said as she smiled and turned to go. "Any time would be good for us. And if you really like old books there's one I'd like you to see. I found it in my grandfather's old trunk, but you know me – I couldn't understand a word of it. Maybe you can get something out of it."

As she walked away the thought loomed as big and obvious to him as the main theme appearing between the lines of so many of the books he'd read: She was in love with him – that's all there was to it. And there was no getting out of having dinner with her.

☙☙☙☙

Her disease, a rare leukemia, advanced so fast that by the time he had an inkling of something wrong it was too late to imagine her surviving it. They had their dinner, and he had The Book before he began noticing that her face was unusually pale. At first he wondered if she was working too long and hard. He had been burning his own share of midnight oil, diverting himself by wrestling with the impossible Latin of the book he had taken home with him, Latin that once-upon-a-time he had known by heart too suddenly lost, slipped away as quietly as his solitary middle-age years.

"I'm tired," he told her once when they met in their coffeeshop. "Sometimes I'm not sure what's wrong with me. And yet I just don't seem to want to sleep. I sit there with that book of yours and try to figure it out, and before I know it the sun's rising and I've barely closed my eyes all night."

"I know exactly the feeling," she said. "It's like day and night are one big ball of string."

"No beginning, middle and end."

"Have you ever tried custard?" she asked. "It always used to work when I was a girl. My mother's recipe."

He tried to arrest her eyes, but she looked away. "You look a little wiped yourself these days. Maybe you could use some of your own medicine."

"Night's my medicine," she said with a sad little smile. "I read all your books at night – sometimes all night. I'll catch up on sleep some other time."

That night he took The Book to bed and opened it in his lap. In the glow of the overhead light its pages seemed yellowed and soft, the printed words meaningless hieroglyphs failing to stand at attention in lines as his eyes passed over them in review. The paper, liver-spotted with age, reminded him of his mother, the soft skin on her arms, and the thick leather binding conjured his father's hands. Mother and father too had come and gone without his having understood more than the barest gist of their lives.

Dolores Johnson's mother made custard for her and passed the recipe on. Dolores Johnson's mother – nameless and faceless. Woman. Like Dolores herself, at once no one and everyone, familiar and strange, her thoughts and intentions unknown, too difficult to unravel and grasp. She seemed hesitant and slow, her mind weighed down by a body that left her breathless every few steps. Only one thing seemed clear: She had overweighed his grasp of life. So he suddenly found himself lecturing directly to her: "Sometimes there's less in a book than meets the eye. Sometimes there's no double or triple meaning to words." And usually, he thought to himself in his darkest moments, words don't make any sense at all.

He closed The Book and put it on the pillow next to himself. Dolores Johnson would not be able to understand a word of it. He wanted to believe otherwise, but in fact she usually did not understand what he was talking about.

"I can't help that," he mumbled as he turned off the light.

を・を・を・を

So there could never be a real meeting of minds.

"Shall we make it a regular thing?" she asked at the conclusion of their first coffee date, weeks before it dawned on him that her skin had an unhealthy hue.

The fact that he still had possession of The Book weighed heavily as the question turned in his mind. If politely he said no, he ought to return it to her; if yes, he might be able to hold on. And one other matter helped make up his mind: she had not yet hinted at the possibility of the impossible – romance.

"That would be nice," he replied. "I haven't done this with anyone for a long, long time."

The truthfulness of his response surprised him more than the fact that he had said yes. He had to admit there was something in it for him besides The Book, something pleasurable about the minutes he had spent with her.

"You seem different," she said, "when you're not in front of the class."

"I suppose I am different. What do you think it is?"

"You don't seem as smart." She laughed. "Did I put my foot in my mouth?"

"And you seem different too – smarter."

"Then let's make it coffee next Friday at eleven again."

He looked forward to it for reasons he did not understand. Again she had carefully prepared her face, the same way she had for their dinner date – the eyes lined in black, the cheeks rouged over, the lipstick laid on thick – the sharp colors ludicrous, even grotesque, when he saw their gloss against his recollection of her naturally pale face.

"Dolores," he began. "The unhappy one."

"Unhappy? Why am I unhappy?"

"I don't know why you're unhappy. Dolor. It's in your name."

"Dolor?"

"Don't you know what 'dolor' means?"

"It sure don't mean dollar bills." She laughed at her own cleverness.

"'Dolor' means unhappiness. Unhappiness is in your name. You're Dolores, aren't you?"

"But that doesn't mean I *have* to be unhappy, does it?"

Her question was full of curiosity. She wanted to know – from him.

"Well, are you unhappy?"

She gave it a long moment's thought. "I'm tired a lot, and maybe I put in a few hours too much at work. But I'm happy, I think. Don't you think?"

"I think it's a matter of definition."

"I really agree. I've got a nice little house, a pretty good job and something special in my life. I'd call that pretty happy, wouldn't you?"

"I would if there's nothing missing that you really want. Is there anything like that – something missing you really want?"

The silence swirled as she looked at herself, confusion crossing her brow.

"I don't think so," she finally replied. "No. But there is one thing."

"What's that?"

"My thoughts are all so mixed up. I have a nosy mind that's always nagging me, if you know what I mean."

He knew what she meant.

"... and I just can't seem to turn it off sometimes."

"I don't think that's such a bad thing," he said.

"And that's why I like to hear you talk. You just seem to have everything figured out. Everything when you say it just begins to make sense."

"You're trying to flatter me."

"No, I'm telling the honest truth."

She wants the impossible, he thought again: She wants me to fall in love with her.

"Because you know I've already got that something special in my life."

"Whatever do you mean this time?"

"You know I'm in love," she said shyly. "I told you Josh loves me a lot. We're going to get married some day. That Josh has a pretty good job, except he's away a lot of the time. He drives a truck and he treats me just wonderful."

෨෮෨෮෨෮෨෮

Most of all he remembered how, in the middle of another sleepless night, his doorbell chimes rang twice. By the time he had his slippers and robe on he saw only the taillights of a car turning the corner away from his house. On the welcome mat at his feet was a small covered dish and a note saying simply, "I thought you might want some of this tonight."

The custard was browned on the edges and still warm, the way he remembered liking it when he was a child. He put the dish on the nightstand next to his bed and opened The Book on the pillow in front of him.

The Book. At that dinner when she first showed it to him he expected much less of her – a cheap old romance, a garage sale item bound in marbled cardboard, the kind of volume that sits unsold for decades on the shelves of antique shops. But when she placed it in his hands a hot flash went through his body, and his legs felt weak. He checked the date twice, just to be sure: 1159 *Anno Domine*. And the title – *Polycraticus: De nugis curialium et vestigiis philosophorum* – almost made sense. By "Iohannes," no doubt some monk or scribe whose steady hand had formed each letter on the page, the first page of every chapter adorned in rich colors by an artist's fine pen. It was a rare and exquisite tome.

"It's some sort of moral treatise," he said.

"Moral treatise?"

"About evil and good. It's beautiful," he said after taking a second look.

"Thank you," she beamed. "It was in my grandfather's old trunk. What language is it?"

"Latin. It seems like Latin to me."

"It's all Greek to me," she laughed. "Why don't you read it and tell me what it's about. Then you can write me a book report," she said laughing again.

"I'd love to try reading it."

"You just take it home with you. Go ahead – it's yours."

"I couldn't just do that."

"Why not? I'm giving it to you."

He chose his words carefully. "I'd want to pay you something for it. It may have some value."

"You take it home and read it first. How do you know? Maybe it's just not a good book."

"No, I don't mean that way. I mean as a thing."

"A thing?"

"A collector's item – something like that."

"You collect books?" she asked.

Her question again rang with genuine curiosity, as if she were asking him if he collected stamps or baseball cards, and why, what was the use of it.

"I don't exactly collect them," he replied, "but I have an eye for good ones that interest me. I... save them, hate to see them get lost."

"Then you should take this one home with you."

"I couldn't do just that. It may have some real value."

"Money? Do you think? How much?"

"I don't really know – and it wouldn't do me any good if I knew."

"Why not?"

"Because I couldn't part with it. I'd never sell a thing like this if I owned it myself."

"If you'd never sell it," she said, her eyes alive with the delight of discovery, "then it isn't worth any money to you. So just take it home with you tonight. I'm giving it to you."

"I couldn't take it just like that."

"As a gift."

"It's too nice."

"Then just hang onto it and read it when you find the time. Then you can tell me what it's about, write me a book report. We can meet for coffee now and then. It's not as if the two of us are going to sit in bed reading it together the rest of our lives."

Until she was very clear about her trucker it didn't occur to him that the "two of us" could have been anyone other than Dolores and himself. At the time the image of being in bed with her struck him as ludicrous, as remote a possibility as it was with the auburn-haired lovely who never looked his way. But later when he found himself in bed, The Book on the pillow close to him, it occurred to him that Dolores too was reading late into the night.

ॐॐॐॐ

What was in it for him – why spend his time with her? At first the same answer kept showing its shameless face: The Book. He would keep having coffee with her because of it, put in his time, enough time perhaps to earn that one-tenth he didn't possess. But one day, after their talk had diminished and disappeared, he finally broke the silence by asking if she no longer wanted to meet with him.

"Oh no, no," she replied. "I really enjoy just being here with you."

He thought of the women he had wooed – how he had to make sure that his words competed successfully against their looks, how often his words had failed. And suddenly a realization – one so simple and obvious that he had looked right past it for years – filled his mind.

"I'm not going anywhere," he said shyly, as if finally alone at an inn with a newly-wed bride.

They kept meeting for coffee, but more and more often she gazed into space. Her skin began to look washed out, a pallid greyishness spreading as the weeks passed. There were moments, some of them falling tonelessly into a bottomless silence, when, looking at her face, he felt as if he were staring at the blankest page.

The terror filled every part of him then. And guilt. This thing that was happening to her was his fault too. He had violated her, done her real wrong, and her body was paying the price.

Then the words in The Book began to weary him, the indecipherable syntax, the whimsical game of musical chairs nouns and verbs were playing to make a fool of him. He put it on his coffee table in the living room, carefully dusting it every three days. Then he tried it between two leather-bound sets of historical works on his shelves, but it seemed lost, invisible there. Finally he settled for a corner of the china cabinet, where it seemed just right next to an antique jade vase.

Now and then he walked by to look at it, and he could think of only one thing to say: "It's beautiful."

෯෯෯෯

It was she who broke the hospital bed silences. The winter seemed unusually long this year, and her fuel bill skyrocketed last month, and Josh was spending too much time on the road and she worried about all the ice and snow, and did anyone ever find the little boy kidnapped three weeks ago from the supermarket parking lot? Words suddenly filled the space between them as they never had before, one word always silently present between the lines: This year's winter was Death, and the fuel bill was Death, and Josh's highway was Death, just as the little kidnapped boy was Death, her Death too.

"I don't understand," she said one day, turning toward the window away from him, "why you come to see me every day."

"And I don't understand," he replied, "what's in it for you. How can I make things up to you? You're the one who invited me to dinner, and you insisted on paying for coffee every time – and then there is that old book you insisted I take home with me. It's maybe worth hundreds of dollars, you know. Maybe more."

She turned toward him. "You're not here because of that."

"Of course not," he said, aware that some part of his response was a lie. And then he told the truth. "You've given me much more than that, and I don't know how to make it up to you."

"I've gotten plenty enough from you."

"What?"

"I told you my mind is a nag. All I have is questions inside of it. Everything – confuses me. You've read all the books. When I listen

147

to you talk you seem to have it all figured out. I don't understand it all, but still it all seems figured out."

"I don't have it all figured out. Sometimes nothing makes sense."

"But you thought about it all – and you aren't afraid. That's why I wanted to get to know you. I used to think about things and begin to get scared. You've thought about everything and you don't seem afraid."

He took her hand. "There's nothing to be afraid of."

"And I was also afraid of you for the longest time."

"Why be afraid of me?"

"I don't know exactly why. I was really confused. Because you never looked at me."

☙☙☙☙

After she died her trucker-lover was inconsolable.

"Things like this don't just happen. Shit is caused. She was just too good. I used to think about her in my truck all the time – just see her there."

He thought about it one more time: Evil. There were many names for it and it showed itself in different forms. It clung to circumstance but was always caused.

He remembered cursing himself the first time he agreed to have dinner at her house. A small pink stucco right at the end of the street. He couldn't miss it if he tried. Was eight o'clock too early or too late? She could change the time for him. And was there anything he couldn't or wouldn't eat? And no, she didn't want him to bring a bottle of wine.

Suddenly he found himself at her door preparing his smile and words. He would have to be at the airport at 10:30 sharp to pick up a friend. He hoped she'd understand.

"I'm so glad to have you here," she said as she let him in. "I wanted you to see my house. Get to know you better, if you know what I mean."

She showed him every room in the house and then photos of her family and friends, and the dinner, glowing in the aura of a candle-lit centerpiece of daffodils, was as exquisite as the wine that loosened his tongue the moment he sat down. Yes, last winter was warm but it was too dry, and he liked gardening even better than reading books, and yes he really liked sports too and he hoped the summer wouldn't be too hot and dry.

"So you read everything I assign?" he asked, folding his napkin to signal that he had had enough.

"Sometimes I read it all again and again," she laughed, "but I don't think it makes any difference. Still I've got a lot of nights with nothing to do, so I just curl up in bed with a book."

He glanced at his watch.

"Sometimes your lover's just not there and it's not his fault," she went on, "and you've got all this time on your hands. And yes – I almost forgot. You said you really love books. The one I wanted you to see. Would you take a look at it?"

"It's beautiful," he said after taking a second look.

"Thank you," she beamed.

"Latin. It seems like Latin to me."

"It's all Greek to me," she laughed. "Why don't you read it and tell me what it's about. Then you can write me a book report."

"I'd love to try reading it."

"You just take it home with you. Go ahead – it's yours."

When he stood outside her door he looked at his watch once more. Seventeen minutes ahead of schedule. His hands were still shaky as he began walking away from her house, glancing over his shoulder to make sure she was not still watching from the porch. The book was a rare and exquisite thing and she *gave* it to him. And he was afraid he would drop it now, a ball possessed by the winning team and the clock running out. He began hurrying with it, his legs nervous and weak, his mind racing as he broke into a run. It was his because she no longer had a right to it, because she was willing to give it up, and because, because, because it would never mean to her what it meant to him. And maybe she would forget, forget about the book, about him, maybe go away somewhere and leave him alone. Yes, she was middle-aged, dumpy, ugly and dumb – she might as well go away somewhere and leave him alone.

# HISTORICAL NOTE ON "WAR STORIES"

"... Hitler had appointed [Reinhard] Heydrich as Governor of the Protectorate of Bohemia and Moravia. Shortly after his arrival in Prague, two young Czechs--Josef Grachnik and Jan Kubis--trained by the British for the express purpose of assassinating Heydrich, parachuted into the Prague area.

On May 29, they ambushed Heydrich as he drove toward Prague, throwing a bomb into his open Mercedes and giving him his death wounds. Both men took refuge inside a crypt in a Prague church. But their associates broke under SS torture and revealed their hiding place. They were seized and executed, after which a wave of terror engulfed the protectorate.

An enraged Hitler bent on avenging the death of the man whom many Nazis believed would be his successor decided that the Czechs must suffer a signal chastisement. Calling for a map of Prague and its environs he put his finger on the village of Lidici and ordered it destroyed. All of the men – most of them steelworkers – were rounded up and murdered, the women were sent to a concentration camp at Ravensbruck and the children despatched to Gneisenau in Germany to be reared as Nazis."

Robert Leckie, *Delivered from Evil: The Saga of World War II.*
New York, Harper & Row, 1987, p. 908.